IMPERFECT TIMING

JESSA HARMON

PROLOGUE

*F*alling in love with Benji had been like slipping into my favorite hoodie. Easy, comfortable, and familiar.

We'd grown up together. We were friends and partners in crime from the time we could walk. One teenaged summer he had caught my attention in a different way. In a way no other boy had before or since.

The rest of my childhood and teenage crushes were only flashes in the pan. They burned hot and quickly fizzled as something or someone else caught my fancy.

Not Benji.

Summer after summer he would visit. Even after he'd left Boston for Scotland each fall, I thought of him often.

Everything changed the summer I turned eighteen. The last summer Benji visited. The last time I saw him.

Falling in love with him had been easy. Getting over him was proving far more difficult.

1

*I*t had been a helluva month.

Between the semester ending and work ramping up, I was dead tired on my feet. The deep circles under my eyes were becoming impossible to hide, even with my best concealer. My friend Carly hadn't outright said anything about my haggard appearance, but she kept giving me sympathy glances in the elevator each morning and her thoughts were always written right on her face. More than once I'd had the urge to put her on the spot and ask her why exactly she was staring at me. But I didn't because she meant well.

My employer, Boston House of Design, had a huge opportunity next month to land an important client. My boss had been on edge for the last few weeks while we put together this proposal for Ball-Barlow International, one of the fastest growing hotel chains in the world. They were considering a complete redesign of about a third of their older hotels, a multi-million-dollar contract for us and a fat bonus for me if we managed to land their business. I had been given a large responsibility for our pitch presentation for the Ball-Barlow executives, which was playing a major role in my current level of mental burnout.

I rubbed my temples as I tried in vain to concentrate on the project plans in front of me, looking up from the blueprints to my computer screen. It was all getting blurry. I was triple checking that I had input all the figures accurately, but my eyes weren't cooperating at the moment. Frustrated, I pushed back my chair and stretched before turning to walk to the office break room in search of coffee. It was mid-afternoon, and I needed my 3pm pick-me-up.

The pot was empty, so I got to work refilling the water and dumped several heaping tablespoons of grounds into the fresh filter. With a snap I turned it on and sat down at the table to wait, inhaling the comforting fragrance as the drip began.

The pot gurgled, and the carafe filled as Peter walked into the break room.

"Afternoon coffee time, Desi?" he asked, his mouth turned up in a sly smirk.

"As usual," I replied.

He turned to regard me carefully, his blue-gray gaze narrowing, "Everything okay?"

I forced a bright smile on my face, but it was clear from his doubtful expression that it wasn't fooling him. "Oh yeah, I'm fine. Just this big client proposal has everyone on edge. I guess I'm not immune to it. Needed a break from staring at the computer screen."

I shrugged and stood. The pot was half full, and I was impatient as always. I pulled it out and poured a steaming cup. I replaced the carafe, and it sizzled on the dripped coffee that had escaped while I poured.

Peter watched me in silence. I raised my cup to him in a farewell gesture and had started toward the door when he finally spoke again.

"Well, it sounds to me like you need a break. Let's have dinner. This weekend, maybe? Take your mind off work?"

I stopped and glanced back at him over my shoulder, attempting to keep the stupidly pleased grin from my face. I was no better at hiding my smile than I was at hiding my exhaustion.

"Peter Grayson, are you asking me on a date?" I turned, tilting my head to the side, which caused my dark curls to fall over my eyes. I didn't add "finally" at the end of my question though it flashed through my head.

"I guess I am, Desi Palmer. So?" He grinned back at me.

I tapped my foot for a moment, making him sweat before I tossed a reply over my shoulder. "Sounds good; Saturday at eight o'clock. Let me know where to meet you."

I exited the break room as he called after me, "Oh, I'll pick you up!"

I returned to my desk and my work, feeling energized for the first time in weeks before even having a sip of my afternoon coffee. What a great end to this stressful Monday.

"I CANNOT BELIEVE he finally asked you out, and it was that lame," Eliza brooded next to me on the sofa at my friend Carly's apartment, painting her fingernails with a satin-y black nail polish. The color only served to further accentuate her alabaster skin. "The break-room? Such a workplace romance cliché."

"She's right, Desi," Meredith said from the floor where she had her most recent legal brief strewn out in front of her, highlighters and pens scattered across the pages. She tossed her long auburn hair over a tanned shoulder. "You've been carrying on this little workplace flirtation for, what? Nine months, now? And that's all he's got?"

"It is not as lame as it sounds," I retorted. "It was sweet and absolutely us."

Eliza rolled her eyes. "Whatever, babe. He's totally getting a catch without having to put in even an ounce of real effort. I haven't met the guy, but he sounds like a dud to me."

I shot a pleading look at Carly and Kira who were cozy on the loveseat opposite us. Kira reading a magazine, her head in Carly's lap as Carly used a pair of tweezers to shape Kira's dark brows. Carly glanced up in time to see my panicked, pleading expression.

"It sounds super sweet, Desi." She winked at me before turning her attention back to Kira's eyebrows.

"He must be dreamy if you are in such a good mood. Because I've got to agree with Eliza on this one, Desi. It sounds lame," Kira chimed in as she tossed the magazine onto the floor. I shot her a glare, and Carly shrugged at me.

"I mean, is this the guy who is finally going to make you forget about–," Eliza started then abruptly stopped herself.

"Make me forget about what?" I asked.

"Nothing, never mind." She flicked her fingers in dismissal, but her brow was furrowed in thought.

"Well, if you guys want to be party-poopers, let's just change the subject," I said.

Eliza sat up and took my face in her hands, the pungent scent of nail polish making me crinkle my nose. "Aww, honey. I'm not trying to rain on your parade. You just deserve the best."

I pouted at her for a moment until she released me. "I know, I know. Just pretend to be happy for me for a few days, okay? At least until after my date. If it's awful, you can all throw him under the bus."

They all murmured in agreement to this stipulation. Kira, brows now finished, sat up. "Let's see a picture. I need to see what we are dealing with here."

I pulled out my cell phone and clicked through a few apps until I came across a good photo of Peter. I turned the phone around and handed it to Kira. She studied the screen carefully for a few minutes, turning it slightly this way and that. She pinched her fingers to zoom in and out. "Is that really necessary?" I asked, an amused smile on my face. "He's a regular guy; what are you trying to find by zooming in?"

"I'm getting an idea of what we are working with here... and here... oh and here..." She smirked as I snatched the phone back. The other women cackled. "He's obviously attractive and from what you've told us about him, seems like a nice guy. I can see why you like him, on paper at least. I mean... do nice guys really ask out girls in the office break room after stringing her along for almost a year?"

"Ha... ha..." I sulked.

"We're only teasing. Remember, we love you," Meredith called from her place on the floor.

"Sure, sure. You say that. You are all good friends... on paper at least."

Carly gasped, offended. "Hey! I totally had your back."

I laughed. "Yes, you did." I stood up and pulled her into a hug. "Thanks, babe."

She smiled and settled back down. "Alright, Kira, my turn for brows."

LATER THAT EVENING I arrived home and made my way to the kitchen for some tea.

I filled the electric kettle and set it on the counter to heat just as my dad walked in.

"Hi there, love. Got enough water for two cups?" he asked.

"Absolutely, Dad." I grinned at him as he took a seat at the kitchen table to wait. I grabbed another mug and tea bag from the cabinet as the kettle came to a boil. I filled both mugs and took them, steaming, to the table. I sat down with him.

"Thanks." He smiled at me, his teeth gleaming white behind his smooth, dark skin. "Hey, I'm glad I caught you, actually. You've been gone so much between work and your classes we haven't chatted in a while."

I smiled warmly at him. "I'm exhausted, but at least there is a light at the end of the tunnel. Next month we will be done with this proposal at work, and I should be able to coast for the rest of the summer, or at least a few weeks." I exhaled in relief. It was nice knowing there was a foreseeable end in sight.

"Oh, that's good. I'm glad things will be winding down for you." He winked. "And that is great timing. We will have a houseguest this summer since your brother is off doing his internship in Las Vegas."

"A houseguest, yeah? Who is that?" I imagined one of my dad's long-lost cousins or uncles or buddies.

"Benji!" He grinned at me as he said the name, obviously excited to give me this news.

I froze, the smile plastered to my face, and I quickly brought my steaming mug to my mouth to hide my shock. Benji? I hadn't thought about Benji in ages. Well, that wasn't quite true. I had thought about him plenty but more in a "remember the boy I was madly in love with when I was eighteen, wonder what he's up to across the ocean" kind of thoughts. Not "he's spending the entire summer in my house" kind of thoughts.

Benji's dad and my dad had grown up together in the Bahamas. Best friends and all that. They had even gone abroad for university together in London. My mother had been studying abroad there as well, all the way from Boston. Benji's mom, Alice, was from the United Kingdom. Edinburgh to be exact. The two couples had been inseparable in their youth. They used to come over to visit almost every summer, and so Benji and I had spent a lot of time together as kids. As teenagers, things had taken a turn...

My mind spun with this news.

"Oh, that's great! What brings him across the pond?" I tried to keep my voice steady. There was no need for Dad to know how this information had sent me spiraling.

"His boss wants him to help start up a new location for the restaurant in the city. He'll be here for a few months to make sure things are running smoothly. He was planning to see if he could sublet an apartment, but I told Joseph we would love to have him here." Dad's grin has stretched across his entire face now. Ear to ear. Dad had always loved Benji. Like another son. Benji was precocious in a way that neither my brother nor I had been. I think he reminded Dad a bit of himself and Joseph when they were growing up in the islands.

"That's great! So, when's he coming?" I sipped my tea.

"He'll be here Thursday."

I choked on the liquid in my mouth. I gasped and wheezed while Dad slapped me on the back, his face now full of concern.

"You okay, love? Desi?"

I coughed again and nodded at him, trying to smile through the tears in my eyes. "Yeah... went down the wrong way."

He smiled again and took a drink from his own mug before he pushed back his chair and stood to go. "I will finish this in the bedroom. It was good catching up, Desi. Take it easy, yeah? You work too hard." He patted me on the shoulder before he turned and disappeared down the hallway, leaving me in silence with my own shocked thoughts.

HIS FACE WAS BEAUTIFUL. It's not one of those things that people say when they are in love with someone, because I was definitely not in love with Benji. It was just a fact; he was beautiful.

A square face with a nicely angled jawline. A smattering of rich brown freckles against the lighter deep gold of his skin. His eyes were somewhere between a green-hazel and amber, always shining with some mischief or joke. He had never been able to keep his feelings from showing right there in his eyes. It annoyed him that he was so transparent. However, annoyance wasn't something you saw in Benji's eyes often or for long. It was usually good-natured twinkling.

And heavens, the accent. If I were ranking the attractiveness of accents, Scots would be at the very top of my list. No question.

He had a way about him that made everyone he encountered feel special. Like they were the only person in the world he cared about. He had surely left a few broken hearts in his wake. Who knew? Seven years had passed, after all.

"Desi? Is that really you, lass?" His voice carried across the terminal.

I could not keep the big stupid grin from my lips as he turned his attention toward me and moved to close the space between us. Eyes shining, his smile widened as he studied me.

"Well, you're all grown up now."

"So are you." I tried not to sway on my feet as he enveloped me in a warm hug, my own arms wrapping around him as I inhaled the still-familiar smell of him, nose buried in his shoulder.

He gripped my shoulders and pulled back, his face inches from mine as he took a closer look at me, the smile on his face softening a bit. "Wow."

"What?" I breathed the question, barely a whisper past my lips. My throat had gone suddenly dry.

Without hesitation, he dipped his head and brought his lips to mine. Warm, urgent. His hands left my shoulders and wrapped around my waist, pulling me closer, pressing me against him. My arms snaked back around him, my palms run across his muscular back as he deepened the kiss and I returned it with fervor. Our breathing quickened together, and just as I felt like I might die from delirious happiness, I heard it.

BEEP, BEEP, BEEP, BEEP, BEEP, BEEP, BEEP, BEEP.

The frantic ringing of my alarm woke me. I was clammy,

disoriented, and a flush of embarrassment crept across my face.

Just a dream, Desi. Just a dream. It doesn't mean anything. It's just Benji.

I swung my arm around to stop the buzzing and rolled back, bringing my hands to my face as I tried to gather my thoughts.

It was just Benji.

2

I had arranged to pick up Benji from the airport.

    I needed a breather at work, and I knew that I wouldn't be able to even beg for time off in the next few weeks as we buckled down to finish this pitch for the Ball-Barlow meeting scheduled for the middle of June.

Consequently, I took a day and a half of my vacation time, and Benji's arrival just happened to be an excellent excuse.

Our CEO prided himself on being hip and up with the times. Taking a "mental health day" was encouraged in the black and white of our employee handbooks, of course. Actually doing it? Not acceptable. They would approve it, grudgingly, but everyone from your immediate supervisor to your coworkers to the HR director then whispered about it behind your back.

And so, the "mental health day wrapped into a "my childhood friend is flying in all the way from London and needs me to pick him up from the airport day" kept the whispers from beginning.

I ended my half-day by having a break-room lunch with

Peter. Things were a little awkward between us since our "big date" was looming in a few days. It was silly to have these butterflies around him at this point. I had spent time with him every day for the last year. We'd had no trouble carrying on flirtatious banter that often toed the line past what was workplace appropriate. Now that we were actually acting on these flirtations, it felt different. The stakes were higher.

He reached out and squeezed my hand as I stood to leave, his fingers lingering just a moment too long to be considered entirely platonic. My face flushed in response, and I pressed his fingers in return, noticing the warmth radiating from his palm.

"You sure you don't want a buddy to ride along with you? I'm delightful company. Not a backseat driver or anything." He'd already asked this question three times today.

"I told you I'm not giving you an out for this meeting, Peter. You're just going to have to suck it up." I grinned as I turned to grab my bag. "Have fun without me tomorrow and I'll see you Saturday. Nine o'clock, right?"

He laughed. "It was eight o'clock, Desi. I'm starting to worry you're going to stand me up."

"Never," I replied with a sly smile. "See you then, Peter."

He waved and strolled back to his desk with a satisfied grin still plastered to his face. It mirrored the one on my lips.

This was good. This was where my attention was best spent.

On the drive to the airport, however, my dream kept replaying in my head. Benji's hands on my shoulders, his lips against mine. Turning up the music didn't help. By the time I pulled into the pickup line, my knuckles were white from the death grip I had on the steering wheel. I pulled out my cell as the traffic slowed and sent Benji a quick text. "I'm here. White Honda SUV. See you soon!"

I tapped my hands against the steering wheel as the line inched forward, and I saw him. His head turned back and forth as he searched the line for my car. My heart hammered in my chest as his amber gaze finally found me and his face broke out into that huge lopsided grin that always seemed to leave me weak in the knees. He waved at me animatedly through the windshield and practically skipped to the door of the SUV.

He hadn't changed in the slightest. I hit the button to unlock the doors, and he reached back to open the rear passenger door to toss in his bag. A huge worn duffle that couldn't possibly contain everything he needed for an entire summer. Typical Benji.

Before I could focus my attention back from the duffle bag, he has slid into the passenger seat beside me and engulfed me in a hug so full of warmth and excitement that I swear my brain forgot how to breathe. I managed to suck in some air and realized that he still smelled exactly how I remembered. My dream came racing back into my mind.

"Desi! It's so great to see you again." He pulled away, releasing me from his embrace, the grin never leaving his face. "It's been way too long, lass. This little mini-vacation is much needed."

My breath caught on the word "lass" as I fought the instinct to remember when I'd last heard that word from his lips. *Not now. Keep your cool, Desi.*

"Opening a new restaurant counts as a mini-vacation these days, Benji?" I asked teasingly, the tight-lipped smile I had forced now softening into a more relaxed expression. "And I thought my bosses were bad."

"Aye, well, I love the restaurant business and getting to

travel is always a treat so I'm still sticking with my mini-vacation comparison." He winked. "If you add up all the hours I'll have to myself, I reckon it would equal at least a few full days of freedom."

I laughed and nodded along. "I guess it would."

"So, what have you been up to lately? I try to keep up on social media, but you aren't nearly as forthcoming with your life as your brother."

"Not everything is important enough to share with the world. On this point Cyrus and I disagree. He wants to share every thought and meal to the masses," I quipped. "Honestly, if he doesn't become some sort of social media influencer in the next few years, I'll be disappointed in him."

"And he's away for the summer in Vegas for his design internship, right?" Benji asked. "That's too bad, I'd like to catch up with him."

"Like you said, Cy will likely be sharing every minute of his summer via Instagram so I'm sure it will be just like seeing him in person."

"So, you've deftly avoided answering my question, lass. What have you been up to?"

"Not avoiding it. My life just isn't that interesting at the moment. I've just finished up my master's program, and I've been working on landing a huge account at work. In a few weeks I should have some loose strings all wrapped up so I can start focusing on the next steps."

For a brief moment I wondered why I hadn't mentioned Peter in this life update.

"And what are the next steps?"

"Well, the big dream goal is to start my own boutique firm. Be my own boss, have my own clients, and be in charge of my own destiny." I said this with a sarcastic lilt in my voice. I was very used to people reacting to this plan of mine in a way that was supportive but still mostly "*yeah, good luck with that*".

"That's amazing, Desi! So, a few years and you'll have that all sorted." Except Benji, apparently.

"Right, long-term, this is more of a five- or ten-year plan. First, it'd be nice to afford to move out on my own. I've been saving and if we land this account, my bonus should get me where I need to be financially to make that happen. Hopefully in the fall I'll have my own place."

"Well, I'm glad you'll be around your parents' this summer at least. It will be great to hang out like old times."

My heart stopped again. This should have been an off-handed comment. After all, we had spent many summers together growing up. But that last summer had changed everything. Surely that's not what he meant. I couldn't bring myself to look at him and instead focused on the highway ahead of me.

"Right, yeah. Like old times," I replied.

We made the rest of the drive back with no further heart-stopping topics of conversation. Mom and dad quickly swept Benji into hugs and conversation, leaving me, thankfully, in the background as they filled the afternoon and evening catching up on life. As early as was polite to do, I excused myself to my bedroom.

Relief coursed through me as the door clicked shut behind me and I collapsed onto my bed. This was going to be more complicated than I thought.

3

$\mathcal{I}$ lay in bed the next morning, enjoying the luxury of being able to wake up slowly. Not having to rush into the city and the office was a pleasant change of pace, and I planned to enjoy every minute since the upcoming month would be very full of work projects.

I stretched lazily before I finally rolled out of bed and padded down the hallway to the kitchen in search of caffeine.

The coffee pot was still warm from when Dad had brewed it earlier this morning, and I poured a generous cup for myself before taking it to the sofa. I sat down heavily, curled my legs underneath me, and grabbed the book I'd been reading from the end table.

One thing I was looking forward to when I started my own design boutique – no more early mornings. I could set my own hours, which meant nothing starting prior to 9:30am. I thoroughly enjoyed beginning my morning with a cup of coffee, relaxing, and reading.

I just finished up my chapter when I heard noises from the kitchen. Benji was awake.

I closed the book and replaced it on the end table before taking my now empty mug back to the kitchen.

"Good morning," I said brightly to Benji. He was standing on tip toes and peering into cabinets, clearly looking for something.

"G'morning, lass. I don't know if you'd happen to know where you keep the tea?" he asked, his voice thick and croaky. It was obvious he was struggling with jet lag.

"Sit, sit. I'll make you a cup. You still take it strong and with milk, yes?" I went to work filling the kettle and gathering the tea bags and milk.

He nodded, not speaking as he sank down into a chair at the kitchen table, his head dropping atop his folded arms. I waited for the water to boil, studying him carefully from across the room. We had spent several hours together, but I hadn't allowed myself to truly see him. He was still lean and long. The gold-brown of his skin glowing against the darker sprinkle of freckles across his neck and shoulders. He had gained more muscle since the last time I'd seen him. Then again, the last time I'd seen him he'd still been mostly a boy. He was now, fully, a man.

He hadn't changed only physically, he even held himself differently. Exuded a confidence I'd never seen in all the years I'd known him. He had grown fully into himself. The same, yet different.

"Why did I think I could have these meetings today, Desi? So stupid. I need a few days to get over this jet lag. It's been so long I'd honestly forgotten how awful it can be."

I dropped two tea bags into the mug of hot water and let it steep as I brought the milk and the mug to the table. I slid into a chair across from Benji. "Is there anything I can do to help? I have the day off."

He raised his head at the smell of brewing tea and met

my gaze. "Erm... maybe? I can't think straight right now. Let me drink my cuppa and then maybe I'll have an answer for you." He poured a generous amount of milk in the cup, not bothering to remove the tea bags, before bringing it gently up to his face for a sip, closing his eyes as he enjoyed it.

"Got to say, lass. This isn't a half bad cup of tea for an American."

I rolled my eyes. "You're welcome, your highness."

He smiled, his eyes still closed. "Thanks, Desi."

"You probably wouldn't feel quite so awful if you weren't also hungover." I smirked at him, and his eyes opened to meet mine over the top of his mug.

"It was just a few drinks with your dad. We had a brilliant time catching up last night." He took another sip, and I knew he really must feel terrible. Usually that bit of teasing would have warranted a clap-back, or a laugh at the very least.

"Yeah, well. You wouldn't have so much to catch up on if you hadn't disappeared off the face of the planet for so long." My tone was light and teasing, but his brow still furrowed at the mention of the length of his absence. Rather than reply he kept sipping his tea, another sure sign that he wasn't faking how awful he felt. "Are you sure you have to meet with these vendors today, Benji? Can't you reschedule?"

He shifted his mug more fully into his left palm so he could rub at his eyes with his free right hand. "Aye, I'll be fine. Just need to get this tea down and wake up a bit more."

I frowned, crossing my arms and biting my lip. Finally shaking my head, I headed down the hall to my room, calling back over my shoulder, "I'm getting dressed and driving you, Benji. You can at least get a little more sleep on the way into the city."

Twenty minutes later we were on the highway and Benji was snoring in the passenger seat while I listened to the local pop radio station at a low volume. It was strange to have him so close after so long and still feel distance between us. As usual during a drive, my mind wandered. It settled on the past I had with the sleeping man next to me. To the last summer he had spent here, right before my last year of high school. Seven years ago. Making this same drive into the city to meet my friends at a music festival.

It was just before everything had changed. When we were just friends who happened to enjoy flirtations and teasing touches. A lingering gaze every so often, maybe. Nothing that crossed the line. Nothing that risked the deep-seated friendship that had been growing since we were babies.

He was just Benji. And I was just Desi. And we were just friends.

It was only a few weeks later that we had fucked it all up. Or I guess I should say I had fucked it all up. And he had gone home. And that had been the end of Benji and Desi.

The DJ's voice blared over the end of the snappy song that had been playing, and it pulled me out of my thoughts. Benji stirred in the seat beside me, scrubbing his hands over his face as he sat up and blinked awake.

"Feeling any better yet?" I asked him and he nodded once, his eyes still droopy but regaining some of their shine.

"Yeah, a little. I think I can make it through this meeting today without really screwing anything up, anyway. The rest of the meetings this week I'll push back to early next week to get a bit more time to settle in and recover." His hands gripped his knees, and he turned to look at me. "Thanks, Desi. You didn't have to waste your whole day off to chauffeur me around, but I do appreciate it. You saved my ass."

I shrugged. "No biggie. It's not like I had some exciting plans you ruined. I only wanted to lounge and read my book, and I can do that just as well in the car while you do what you need to do." I nodded at the spine of a book peeking out of my bag and he reached down to pull it out.

"What're you reading anyhow, lass? Let's see." He grinned and flipped open the book to read the blurb on the inside cover. "Will love really conquer all for Theodora and her fated prince?" He read the final line aloud and raised an eyebrow at me.

I threw my head back and laughed, but my cheeks flushed pink. "A girl can dream, can't she?"

"I guess that depends whether you're actually hoping for that kind of happy ending or if you're just using it as an excuse to keep people away." He smiled, but his brow furrowed.

"Whoa, that's some deep stuff there, Benji. Point out the woman who hurt you so I can kick her ass." I nudged his elbow playfully and his smile faded, his gaze turned back to my face, and my chest tightened at the strange look he gave me. A serious Benji was something I hadn't seen often and the intensity behind his eyes made my stomach flip anxiously. "What?"

"I don't think that'll be necessary, Desi. Probably not possible anyhow." His lips curved up into a smile again and in an instant, he is back to typical Benji. "Would be an interesting thing to witness, however."

We'd made it downtown, and I pulled the car into a parking garage and found a well-lit spot near the back. Benji gathered his things and leaned into the car one last time. "An hour tops, lass. Enjoy your book in the meantime. Hopefully that Prince Charming is all you've ever dreamed he could be." He winked and disappeared.

I took a deep breath as I allowed the silence to fall around me. My hand rested against my chest where my heart still hammered wildly. Not even here for twenty-four hours and already he had me completely confused.

I took a swig from my water bottle before reaching down to grab my book and I settled in, the breeze coming through the parking garage and my open windows creating a nice enough atmosphere that I barely even noticed I was cramped in my car on my last day of freedom for the foreseeable future. I was so engrossed in the story when Benji returned that the sudden violent opening of the car door made me jump.

And there was my heart hammering away again.

"Dammit, Benji. You scared the crap out of me."

He grinned and settled into the passenger seat. "Sorry, lass. Didn't mean to interrupt your time with Prince Charming."

"You aren't going to let that go, are you?" I asked.

"Never," he replied. "I'm starved; is that little diner near your parents' house still in business?"

I nodded. "Of course. Frank is never giving up on that place. Lunch, then?"

"Definitely. I can already taste the milkshake." He rubbed his hands together in glee, and we get back on the road.

The drive back was night and day different from the previous journey. Benji was awake, for one, and he had a way of making light and easy conversation that made the time pass quickly and pleasantly. He got me talking about my dream of starting my design firm and seemed genuinely excited about the ideas I had.

"You are going to be brilliant at that, Desi. Seriously. What's the plan? Get a year or two under your belt and establish yourself a bit before setting off on your own?" he asked, and he was openly curious.

So many of the people I talked to about this dream of mine scoffed or played the devil's advocate role when discussing it with me. People were supportive, obviously, but there was always an underlying tone of doubt and of "just stick with the sure thing". Being employed was safe. It was a consistent income. Starting off on your own was an enormous risk, and one that I felt fully capable of taking on my shoulders. But it was hard not to feel discouraged by well-meaning friends and family talking about "harsh realities".

"Well, maybe more like five years. I don't know." I shrugged off the question, and he placed a hand on my arm.

"Lass, you could definitely do it now if you wanted. I can understand wanting to get some security in place first, though. Like you said yesterday, you want to move out of your parents' house first, aye?" He gave my arm a gentle squeeze before settling his hand back on his leg. "I'm in the same boat, anyway."

"You are?" I asked, eyeing him from across the car.

"Yeah. I'd much rather work for myself. I'd rather be running a bakery than a restaurant. But the money is good, and it's not my neck on the line, right?" He smiled a little sadly. "I'm trying to figure out how to convince Hank that it would be an outstanding idea for him to partner with me on opening it."

I laughed. "Convince your boss to give you money when you quit?"

He chuckled. "I suppose when you put it that way... I don't know. I've not got a real head for business anyhow. I didn't go to a fancy university like you did."

"You can hire people to take care of that kind of stuff, Benji. I know your baked goods are amazing and inventive. I doubt there's another place out there that does what you could do with your own place."

I pulled into a parking space at Frank's Diner, but I didn't turn off the ignition just yet, my gaze meeting Benji's serious face. So much serious stuff happening with him today. It was throwing me off.

"And I'm not just saying that because you'd surely give me free cupcakes," I finished finally.

The joke broke the tension, and he laughed, moving to open his door as I turned off the ignition and followed him inside where we immediately headed for the same booth we always had as teenagers.

We'd just ordered when the door swung open once more and Kira and Eliza strolled in. Eliza spotted us immediately and hurried over, flinging her long pale arms around Benji's neck.

"Ah! I can't believe it's you! It's been WAY too long, mister." She settled in beside him and Kira slid in next to me and for a moment it was like we were eighteen again. Benji, however, wasn't blushing beet red from the attention he had just received. He warmly accepted the hug and got right to the catching up. He had always gotten along well with my friends. Though he'd never bothered flirting with them, it had always left his cheeks flushing when they showed him any sort of interest.

Not everything was the same, then.

"So, Desi told us you are opening a new restaurant?" Kira asked, and Benji nodded.

"Aye. The London location is doing well, and my boss Hank knew I had some ties to Boston, so here I am." He grinned. "You ladies come by anytime, and I'll give you a free appetizer."

"Oh, I'll definitely take you up on that offer," Kira said with a wink. "When's the opening?"

"Well, we have already worked a lot of the preliminary details, so it's just putting some finishing touches on the location and hiring some staff. I'm hoping three weeks and we will be up and running." He was practically buzzing with excitement.

Eliza smirked. "You haven't changed a bit. I'm questioning your boss's decision to send you on such a big project."

Benji clutched his hand to his chest as though he'd been wounded, and she elbowed him playfully. "I'll be there opening night if there's even a table open. You'll kill it. I still haven't had a cupcake that tops the ones you made for Desi's eighteenth birthday."

We spent the rest of the meal chatting, laughing and reminiscing. As we were wrapping up, Benji mentioned we should all go get drinks the next evening.

"I would even have said right now, but this jet lag has knocked me on my arse and I'm looking forward to a nap."

I shifted uncomfortably. "Sorry, Benji, I've got plans for tomorrow night already."

"Oh, right! Your date with Mr. Office Romance." Kira smiled and tapped her finger to her chin. "I'm free tomorrow, Benji. What about you, Eliza?"

Eliza nodded enthusiastically. "Yep! Harvey is still working late nights, prepping to open the new tattoo shop, so my night is completely free. We've gotta introduce you to Juno's, Benji! It'll be fun to get some drinks with you. Desi will just have to miss out."

I thought I noticed Benji's face tense for a moment but if it did, he regained his composure so quickly that I wasn't sure I had seen it after all.

"I'll get your numbers from Desi then and catch up with you tomorrow." He leaned forward to hug them both warmly. "So great to see you two again."

We said our goodbyes and headed back to my car.

"A date, then, lass? I didn't realize you had a boyfriend." He asked the question casually, but his eyes weren't shining like they normally did.

I nodded. "It's very new. First date."

I shrugged it off, swallowing hard and trying to ignore the tightness that appeared in my chest. I refused to dwell on what that feeling meant.

"Right. Cool. I'm glad it's not too weird for me to go out with your friends without you. It's really as though no time has passed since I was here last." He stretched and yawned. "I could go for that nap now."

"Your wish is my command. Let's get you back to bed."

4

_I_n the hall bathroom Saturday evening, with piles of discarded clothes around my feet and the countertop strewn with hair and beauty products, I carefully applied my makeup for my date with Peter. I didn't go all out with my day to day look like Eliza did, but this was a special occasion. I decided on a dress that was a little too short and a little too low cut to be work appropriate but still fit into the "classy" category rather than all out "sexy". The soft blush color contrasted nicely against my darker skin. I pinned my curls back with a few of them falling out loosely to frame my face. Even though Peter saw at work every day, he hadn't seen me like this.

I was finishing up my smokey eye when Benji rounded the corner to step into the small pace before he stopped short. He ended up mere inches from me and his hands reflexively reached up to grasp my elbows, steadying himself. My heart squeezed at the sudden physical proximity.

"Sorry, Desi. I didn't realize you were in here." He took a step back, his hands dropping back to his sides as I tried to regain my composure. His eyes scanned the bathroom, an eyebrow raised. "Was there a tornado I missed?"

I rolled my eyes, letting the intensity of my confused feelings fade away. "Do you need the toilet? I'm about done here."

His amber gaze settled on me again, an expression on his face that I almost recognized before it was replaced with his usual mischievous smirk. "That's okay, I'll go downstairs." He stepped back again, into the hallway. "You look really nice. Lucky guy."

He disappeared and my face flushed hot once more. *It's just a compliment, Desi. It's just Benji. Pull it together.*

I made work of cleaning up my mess, putting away the hair products and makeup and gathering my discarded outfits in my arms before I headed back to my bedroom. I closed the door and leaned against it, tossing the mound of clothes onto my bed to deal with later. Or tomorrow. Or not at all, judging by the floor of my closet. I wasn't a slob, really. I just didn't see the vital importance of putting clothes in place when I was going to wear them again, anyway.

I stepped over to my dresser and put on the silver earrings and necklace lying on top, then leaned down and picked up the pair of peep toe booties I had chosen to go with the dress before I made my way to the kitchen. My mom spotted me from her place at the stove as I entered the room.

"Honey, that boy will fall over when he sees you." She set her spoon on the counter and stepped toward me with her arms wide. I returned her hug. "Just beautiful. You should wear that dress more often."

"Thanks, Mom." I grinned and settled into one of the kitchen chairs to put on my shoes.

"So where is he taking you?" she asked, returning to her

task of cooking dinner. It smelled amazing, some kind of buttery shrimp dish with pasta.

"I'm not sure, actually. He just said he'd pick me up at eight o'clock and to wear something a little dressed up," I answered. It was nice not having to make the plans for once. In my group of friends, that task usually fell to me or Carly.

I checked the time and my stomach flipped. He would be here any minute. I shouldn't be nervous. We knew each other very well already, even if this was our first official date. But it was still unfamiliar territory.

My dad strolled into the kitchen. He wrapped his arms around my mom's waist and kissed her neck affectionately. "That smells heavenly, Vera."

Mom batted him away with a grin. "It's not ready yet. Go talk to your daughter and stop distracting me."

Dad threw up his arms in defeat, but his smile widened, and he turned to take a seat next to me. "Date tonight, then?" he asked, taking in my outfit with wide eyes. It wasn't exactly a disapproving look, but I knew he'd rather I had chosen something more modest. He was wise enough to keep that opinion to himself, however.

"Yep! He should be here any minute." I checked the clock again before my gaze fell to the stairs. "Where'd Benji get to? I'd have thought his nose would have led him here by now."

"Eliza and Kira came by about fifteen minutes ago to pick him up," my mom answered, pulling plates from the cabinet for herself and my dad.

Right. I had forgotten they had made plans to go out together tonight. A knock echoed down the hall and I sprang to my feet, but my dad was already striding out of the room. I rolled my eyes and followed him. My mom wiped her hands on the kitchen towel, grinning, and trailed after us.

Dad had the door open already, and I caught sight of Peter over his shoulder. He was shaking my dad's hand and smiling when his eyes fell on me. His expression changed, and his smile softened. My cheeks grew hot at the appreciative look on his face. He was wearing a crisp white button down, sleeves rolled up over his elbows, and a pair of nice navy slacks. It was similar to what he wore to the office on a daily basis, but casual in a way that made my stomach flip again.

"Are you ready, Desi?" he asked after making pleasantries with my parents and I nodded, stepping forward to take his offered hand.

"Of course, let's go." I smiled and glanced at my parents as they nodded their approval before following Peter to his waiting car for our first official date.

"I DON'T THINK I can fully explain in words how amazing it was." I sighed, falling back against the sofa cushions in Kira's apartment. Sunday brunch was one of our traditional fab five get-togethers, though they had become more infrequent as our lives evolved. We were missing Meredith, whose current job at a prominent law firm left her with very little in the way of work-life balance.

"So where did he take you?" Eliza pressed, leaning forward with her chin in her hands.

"We went into the city to this tiny little Italian restaurant. The food was amazing, and they had this little private terrace with fairy lights and candles. It was so nice to spend time with him outside of the office setting. It made the flirting more exciting somehow." I bit my lip, and Eliza's smile widened.

"You mean because you might actually be able to act on it?" she teased, and Kira laughed.

I huffed and rolled my eyes at her before Carly piped up. "That sounds dreamy, Desi."

"Thank you for being the only one who can keep her mind out of the gutter, Carls." I leaned over and hugged her tightly. "After dinner we went to this rooftop bar that over-looks the harbor and found a table where we could take in the view and the lights. We had some drinks and just talked for so long."

"Okay, Desi. Love the fairytale stuff, but seriously, can you get to the steamy parts?" Kira sighed.

"He brought me home, and we had a nice kiss goodnight in the car. Is that what you wanted to know?" I replied, irritation clear in my tone. "You know I don't do the big stuff on a first date, Kira."

She smiled a knowing smile and nodded. "I know that, but with as much as you've been gushing about the guy, I thought you might change things up this time around."

I remembered the kiss I had shared with Peter the night before. His hand slid up my bare thigh, my arms wrapped around his neck, pressing myself close to him. The smell of his cologne and the taste of wine in his mouth. How it had been him that had pulled away, resting his forehead against mine as my heart pounded in my chest and I thought about how much I wanted to straddle him right there in the car in front of my parents' house.

"I've got to leave you wanting more, yeah?" He had grinned, kissed me softly once more and turned to leave the car, walking around to open my door for me and help me out. He walked me to the door, leaned down to whisper in my ear, "I'll see you Monday."

I would not admit it to my friends. But I would have taken things further. Absolutely. And that for once in my life it had been the man who resisted, who had put on the brakes, who had respected my space... just made me want him that much more.

"It was a great date, and I honestly cannot wait for the next one." I finished. And for the first time since the Scotsman had reappeared in my life, Benji's face didn't flash into my mind next to Peter's.

5

---

*L*ater that afternoon, I dug through the drawer on my end table for the third time, huffing in frustration.

"Where the fuck is it?!" I exclaimed and shoved the drawer closed again.

I was on the hunt for my college transcripts. Human Resources had requested them after they completed a records audit and found they either never had copies or had misplaced them at some point. I had already torn my room apart trying to find them. I flung myself down in my bed, my brow knitted as I tried to remember the last time I'd seen it. It had been a while.

Finally, I decided it must be on one of the boxes I never unpacked once I moved back home following undergrad two years ago. I groaned at the thought of trudging all the way up to the apartment over my parents' garage to dig through boxes, but I needed these for work the next day and I really didn't want to have to pay new copies if I didn't absolutely have to.

I stood and headed over to the apartment. The metal

stairs complained with low creaks as I trudged up them, and I grimaced at the chipped paint and rust spots.

My parents had decided to renovate the space above their garage and turn it into an apartment for some extra income when I was in college. They actually made some headway on the project and then changed course to offer me the space once I graduated. I would complete some of the manual labor and add some finishing touches as well as make final design decisions in exchange for paying a minimal rent and utility overhead for a few years until I could get on my feet financially.

Unfortunately, in the midst of this, my dad had lost his job. They couldn't afford to finish the apartment and were barely able to make ends meet for their regular expenses. So, I had moved back home to help. It was a benefit to both of us, really. I could save money on rent for a while and help my parents keep their house while my dad got back on track.

I unlocked the door and pulled the metal folding chair from inside toward me, propping it in the doorway so it wouldn't latch while I searched. This had a dual purpose of allowing some air flow as well as the inside door handle tended to stick, and I'd been trapped up here more than once because of it. It was such a simple fix, but it simply wasn't a priority; none of us needed to come here often anyway.

I took a moment to look around. The like-new white cabinets and small kitchen island were covered in a layer of dust. The sleek, dark hardwood floors were still covered with a protective cardboard layer and various materials were still piled around. Boxes of tile for the kitchen back-splash and the bathroom shower. Stacks of white base-boards and other trimmings. My parents had purchased nearly all of the materials before it all came crashing down.

I inhaled deeply as I thought of how the last few years might have been different. I would have been living here, in my own space. I would have been putting my skills as a designer to work on this place, without the corporate restraints, and had a head start on building my portfolio for my own firm. Nothing I designed at BHD was truly mine, per my contract. It was the intellectual property of the company.

I shook my head and turned my attention to the stack of plastic totes in the center of what would have been the living room and headed over to resume my search. They had to be here somewhere.

Footsteps rattled the metal staircase, and a moment later Benji appeared in the doorway.

"Hey, lass! I was just wondering if you knew where your mom's stand mixer was. I'm going to make some cookies."

He lifted the chair from the doorway and stepped inside as he spoke. I turned around just in time to see the door closing.

"Benji! No!" I shouted. But it was too late, the latch clicked shut.

Benji raised his eyebrows, his forehead wrinkled. "What?"

I huffed then groaned. *Fuck.*

"The door doesn't open from inside, Benji. That's why I had the chair sitting there."

Benji reached over and tried the door handle as I pulled out my phone and dialed my mom's number. She'd been having to go into her firm's office on weekends for the last few weeks as they'd had someone quit unexpectedly. Only after the previous employee had gone had the firm's owner realized they'd left their accounts in a complete mess. Mom was helping clean it up.

"I'll just go out the window and open it from the outside," Benji suggested, and I shook my head vigorously.

"No, you can't. None of the window's open to the roof, and you are *not* jumping from a second-floor window," I replied.

"Hello?" My mom answered her phone. I quickly explained our situation.

"Shit, sorry, baby. I can't get out of here until at least dinnertime, the situation here is such a mess. Can you wait that long?"

I sighed. "That's fine, Mom. We can survive a few hours."

As I said this, I met Benji's mischievous gaze and my stomach flipped in response. It was just a few hours. I could handle this. It was just Benji.

Quickly averting my eyes, I said my goodbyes to my mother. I clicked to end the call and set phone on the counter before I turned to open a window. It was already warm outside, and the air in the apartment was stuffy, but I was pretty sure my sudden sensation of suffocation had less to do with my physical circumstances and more to do with the idea of spending hours trapped in this small space with Benji and all of my jumbled thoughts and feelings about him. I threw up the window and leaned out slightly, filling my lungs with the slightly crisper early summer air outside.

"Are you claustrophobic, lass?"

Benji's voice behind me made my stomach twist again. I took a final deep breath before pulling my head back inside and shaking my head at him.

"No, but I already worked up a sweat looking for these damn transcripts and I need the extra airflow. Can you open that one too? Should get a good enough breeze with them both cracked." I gestured toward the window behind him and then returned to the stack of totes.

Benji opened the second window obediently.

"Need a hand?" he asked. "It's the least I can do for getting us stuck up here."

"Sure, you can dig through that stack there. They should be in a black folder somewhere."

Benji popped open the lid on the first box and pulled out a folder.

"This?" He held it up.

I stepped forward to take it from his hand and flipped the folder open. "Yep, that's it."

Of course he would find it immediately. So much for distracting myself with the search. I settled myself onto one of the dusty bar stools at the kitchen island, tossing the folder on the counter as I did.

"Guess now we just wait."

I was already sweaty and clammy. I pulled my curls up off my neck and secured them in a bun on top of my head with a hair tie from my pocket. Benji watched me, an amused smirk on his face.

"What?"

He shrugged. "Dunno, you're acting all funny."

"How do you know this isn't how I always act? It's not like you really know me anymore," I retorted.

I immediately regretted the words. The last thing I wanted was to spend these hours rehashing our past. He raised an eyebrow at me but said nothing.

"Sorry, that was uncalled for. I'm just really stressed at work with this big presentation coming up, and now on top of everything, I'm hot and sweaty and trapped up here which is always a reminder of how things didn't work out as

I'd planned." I waved my arm at the half-finished room as I spoke, and hot tears sprang to my eyes.

What the hell? Why was I crying all of a sudden?

I tried to blink them back, but one traitorous drop slipped down my face. I closed my eyes and swallowed hard, trying to maintain control.

When I opened them again, Benji had moved closer. His long fingers rested on the counter beside mine and I could smell the clean pine scent of his soap as the breeze from the window brushed past him. His brow was furrowed, and his expression was impossible to interpret. He'd always been so hard for me to read. He looked as though he wanted to say something but then he simply reached down to grab my other hand from my lap. He gave my fingers a reassuring squeeze, his hand warm and firm against mine.

It was just a normal hand. It was simply a friendly, supportive gesture. So why did my skin burn where his hand met mine? And why were sparks of heat shooting up my arm? Why did my heart stutter in my chest? It was just Benji.

This was becoming my mantra, but the truth was he had never been just Benji.

I swallowed again and breathed slowly and carefully as the knot twisted more tightly in my chest before it slowly loosened and faded along with the threat of tears.

"The way this shook out wasn't your fault, Desi. It wasn't anyone's fault. It was just shitty luck."

I nodded. Logically I knew this to be true. But that didn't keep the irrational anxious worries away completely. "Thanks, Benji."

"Anytime."

His crooked grin lacked its usual hint of mischievous

humor when I finally managed to look him in the eye again. His brow was furrowed with something like concern and his eyes held a sadness that was deeper than this little exchange warranted. I shifted in my seat and finally broke eye contact.

I patted the stool next to mine. "Might as well sit down. Mom won't be here for at least another hour."

He settled next to me, facing out so he could lean back on the counter. His elbow brushed my arm as he made himself comfortable. My cheeks grew hot, and I dug my nails into my palm to focus on something other than how these fleeting and innocent touches were evidently causing my brain to misfire.

"So how was your hot date last night?"

He asked the question casually enough, but I thought I noticed an unusual tightness in the set of his jaw, and his smile didn't sparkle all the way up to his eyes as it normally did.

"It was nice. Peter is a really good guy, and this date has been months in the making," I replied. I thought he winced briefly at this, but I must have been imagining things. There was no reason me going on a date with Peter should have any impact on Benji. "How was Juno's with the girls?"

He sat forward on the stool, his grin widened, and the twinkle returned to his eyes.

"Oh, it was mad. Eliza was absolutely steaming, and Kira and I spent the whole night making sure she didn't wander off. It was almost like Kira and I were parenting a foul-mouthed toddler." He laughed and recounted the whole evening in vivid detail, which had me in tearful stitches by the end. It felt good to laugh with him.

After our laughter subsided, the silence grew again. A silence filled with electric tension as I met his gaze, my lips still curved in a smile. His golden eyes drew me in, and I realized at some point during our conversation my hand had migrated so close to him on the counter that my thumb was brushing against his freckled arm. Flutters started again in my stomach, and a hot flush rose on the back of my neck.

I thought his eyes flickered down to my mouth for a moment, but it was so quick I couldn't be sure. I licked my lips at the thought, then pressed them together and with deliberate effort I turned my face away from him. Though I couldn't quite move my hand away from his warmth. Not yet.

"I've missed you, lass," Benji said finally. His voice was low and gruff. I pressed my eyes closed for a moment grappling with what exactly he meant by this. Did he mean he missed spending time with me as his friend? Or did he mean he missed what we became so briefly? It was not a conversation I was mentally prepared to have right now.

"I missed you too. Next time don't stay away so long," I said, a playful lilt in my voice and a forced smile on my lips. I finally moved my hand and placed a playful smack to his shoulder. This did the trick and we both shifted in our seats, the heaviness dissipating as if it had never been there. Maybe it hadn't. Maybe it was just in my head.

Just me romanticizing and imagining things again.

"I'll do my best," he said. His smile had returned, though I noted it wasn't as bright as when he'd been telling me about babysitting drunken Eliza.

The metal rattle of footsteps on the stairs echoed outside and I stood, itching to get out of this apartment and put some space between me and Benji. I needed to clear my head. Being this close to him got my thoughts all muddy.

"Oh good! Mom's here."

A moment later the door opened, and my mom's scowling face appeared. She stood a moment, her hand on her hip as she passed her gaze between the two of us. "Why is it that when the two of you are together you always seem to end up in messes like this?"

Benji laughed and shrugged. "Probably some sort of sign. Right, Vera? I'll make you some cookies as atonement if you'll tell me where you keep your mixer."

She rolled her eyes and smirked at him, though I could see the good humor in her expression. She took a step back to hold open the door. "Well, come on now, you've been rescued. I need to eat and head back to the office for a few more hours."

"Thanks, Mom," I said as I made my way through the doorway behind Benji.

Her sharp brown eyes narrowed at me for a moment, but then she smiled thinly. "You're welcome, baby. Just try not to let this happen again."

6

---

*T*he restaurant was bustling. There was a small crowd of people milling around outside on the sidewalk waiting for their tables when the five of us arrived. I gave my name to the hostess, and she hustled us back to the small private room and I made a mental note to thank Benji for that extra touch later.

We were settling into our seats after ordering our first round of cocktails when I heard them coming, a giant cupcake complete with an enormous candle leading the way as the four of them approached our table.

I gritted my teeth. "I'm going to kill him."

My friends laughed, clapped, and cheered along with the song before the restaurant staff set the cupcake in front of me and departed. I hid my face in my hands. "That was so embarrassing."

Carly elbowed me from her place at my side. "Oh, lighten up, Desi! It's your birthday. Have some fun." She raised her drink and the rest of my friends followed suit. "To Desi!"

They echoed her sentiment and Kira added, "And to supporting Benji with his newest venture."

We drank to that and then ordered nearly every appetizer on the menu, chatting and drinking while the restaurant bustled along around us.

The food was delicious. Hot and expedient. The staff was a well-oiled machine already, even on opening day. There were no hiccups, and most of the other patrons seemed to be quite pleased with the service and the food. It impressed me how well Benji had pulled this off.

I hadn't given him enough credit. My brain still had him filed away under "childhood love" rather than an actual fully fledged and competent man. He was good in the kitchen. He had proven that even as a teenager. But managing a full restaurant staff, and opening a location on his own? I was in awe of him.

"So, Desi, how are things with Mr. Workplace Romance?" Meredith asked, taking a sip of her sangria.

I brightened at the mention of Peter. "It's going so well. I'm almost afraid that he's too perfect. Like maybe he's secretly a serial killer."

The girls all laughed. We were well into our third round of drinks.

"Well, where is he tonight? Not ready to do the whole birthday thing with you yet? Is that too serious for him?" Eliza asked, pouting a bit. She was getting impatient about the fact that he hadn't yet met any of my friends.

"He's out of town this week. Visiting some family in Vermont. I think a cousin's wedding or something?" I shrugged. "Either way, something he'd committed to long before he knew my birthday would be a factor in his life. I needed some girl time, anyway. I've missed you guys!"

I wrapped my arms around Carly and Eliza, squeezing

them tightly as they closed our circle with Kira and Meredith, and we all leaned forward together in our group hug.

"It's time for us to meet this boy of yours, Desi. I mean, I know I've seen him around the office but that's not the same," Carly stated after we've released one another. "Oh! I'll have a party next weekend! You can all come, and Peter can meet us all at once!"

Everyone nodded their agreement, and we set the plans for the next weekend.

"Speaking of past due introductions," Meredith started, "Carly and I are starting to feel a little left out of all of this Benji to-do."

Carly sulked and nodded. "It's true. I've heard so much about him, but he has yet to grace us with his presence."

"Well, let's fix that then, shall we?" I said, the alcohol having already dulled my discretion or sense of boundaries. Normally I wouldn't have dreamed of doing this to him during his big opening night. I waved down a passing waitress. "Can you tell Benji we need to speak with him? There was a problem with one of the appetizers."

The waitress nodded solemnly and headed off to the kitchen while the others stared at me wide-eyed. "Desi! He's going to freak out." Kira scolded. I laughed and waved her off.

"It'll be fine. Consider it payback for the birthday cupcake embarrassment."

A few minutes passed before the Scotsman appeared, his expression serious and concerned before he finally looked up and saw the group seated at the offending table. He quirked a brow at me. "I'm told there was a problem?"

I grinned at him. "Yes. The appetizers were too delicious. It should be illegal. Also, the cupcake was embarrassing, and I wanted to file an official complaint."

He smirked at me before turning his attention to Carly and Meredith. "This must be the two missing members of the fab five I've heard so much about." He reached out and offered his hand to each of them. "It's nice to finally meet you two."

He returned his attention to me. "I'm terribly sorry for the unfortunate birthday celebration. I assure you it won't happen again." He winked. "And how are you getting home, birthday girl?"

Eliza raised her hand. "Designated driver here."

Benji nodded in approval. "All right, good. As it's clear she's in no condition to drive herself."

I scoffed, and he grinned again. "Have a pleasant rest of your evening, ladies. I do hope that the too-delicious appetizers do not ruin your night."

And with a wave and a wink, he was gone.

"I'M LOOKING FORWARD to finally meeting your friends, Desi." Peter reached over and grabbed my left hand from my lap, lifting it to his face to brush his lips across my knuckles. "I kind of feel like I know them all already, though." He winked, a smirk on his handsome face.

"They are really looking forward to meeting you too. I just hope they don't scare you off," I teased.

"Good thing I don't scare easy."

This felt so natural and right and good. It's easy and light. Just like it's always been, except now he was officially mine.

This party that Carly was hosting was our fourth "date" and things had been going well, if uneventful, since our first dinner together a few weeks ago.

Granted, the Benji complication was still in the mix. But I was confident I was almost past that entire thing. He was only here for a few months anyhow, and I had been working so much on the Ball-Barlow International design project and he had been in the city so often, working late hours preparing for the restaurant opening and subsequent first week of business that we hadn't even seen each other except in passing since that afternoon trapped in the apartment. It would be fine.

"So is your house guest making an appearance tonight?"

I stiffened at the casual mention of Benji breaking into my thoughts of him.

"Oh... um. I don't know. He and Kira and Eliza have kind of hit it off, so one of them might have invited him?" That was a bit of an understatement, really. They loved Benji. He fascinated them. And they had taken it upon themselves to make sure he had a good time while he was on this side of the pond. Something my brand-new relationship and work schedule wasn't really allowing me to take point on.

Why hadn't I considered that Benji might be here tonight?

We pulled up to the high rise where Carly and her boyfriend Liam lived, finding a parking spot just down the street. We were running late, so everyone else was surely already inside.

Peter grabbed my hand as we strolled into the building. We stood waiting for the elevator and a familiar voice called out from behind us.

"Fancy meeting you here."

My face was flushed hot before I even looked at him.

He is grinning when I turned around, his hazel eyes passing with mild curiosity between me, Peter, and our entwined fingers. "Oh, Benji! Hi! We were just wondering if you would be here!" My voice sounded weird. Too bright, too eager. Benji's grin settled into an amused smirk, an eyebrow rising. He had noticed.

"Aye, Kira invited me. I just finished up at the restaurant and it's only a bit of a walk from here. I figured, why not?" He turned his attention to Peter. "Nice to meet you, mate. Peter, I'm guessing? Desi's mentioned you a few times."

He held out a hand which Peter grasped firmly with his free palm. His other hand gripped my fingers more tightly.

"Pleasure. I've heard about you as well."

The elevator dinged and the three of us stepped into the compact space. Benji leaned casually against the wall beside me. They made small talk on the way up to Carly's floor while I stood awkward and quiet between them.

"How are you finding Boston?"

"Well, it's not London, but I suppose there are worse places."

"And you're a chef?"

"Aye, finished up culinary school last year but I've been working for Hank Torrance at his restaurant in London since I finished secondary. His stipulation for letting me spread my wings and open a new location was to finish my schooling so that's what I did."

Finally, we reached our floor and I slipped through the doors before they've even fully opened.

"Whoa, Desi. You in a hurry?" Peter teased me as I pulled him out behind me and practically barreled down the hall to Carly's apartment.

"It's been a long week. I really need some girl time and alcohol," I joked with a light laugh. It felt forced.

I tapped cursorily on the door before opening it and stepping inside. Peter and Benji slipped in behind me.

"Desi!" A unison shout from the girls as they made their way toward us, and I made all the usual introductions.

"Peter, this is Carly, Eliza, Meredith, and Kira. The rest of the fab five." I beamed at my friends as I watched them sizing up my date approvingly.

Kira smiled and reached out to run her hand across Peter's bicep before giving his arm a squeeze. "I think he'll do, Desi." She grinned at me then turned to Benji, opening her arms for a hug which he readily accepted, pressing her close.

I felt a twinge of jealousy at their closeness, but I shook it off. Kira knew how I felt about Benji. She was one of my oldest friends. She would never do anything to jeopardize our relationship. Would she?

Ignoring this for now, I returned my attention to the other three women and Peter who was looking at me with an eyebrow raised. "I am dying for a drink. Carly? Gin?"

She beamed and grabbed my hand, pulling me to the kitchen to make me a drink. I glanced back at Peter and winked. He returned the gesture before returning his attention to Meredith and Eliza for polite introductory conversation.

"Oh. Em. Gee. Desi! You have not done him justice even in all of your gushing about him over the last few months." Carly went right to work making me a drink as her boyfriend Liam stepped into the kitchen to grab another beer from the refrigerator.

"Hey, babe." He affectionately drew a hand across Carly's lower back, pressing a kiss to the side of her head as he moved past her. "Desi! Is that your new fella over there being grilled by Eliza and Meredith?"

I nodded, grinning. "His name is Peter."

"Poor guy. You'd better not leave him too long, those two

are terrifying." He laughed, popping the cap off his bottle of craft beer before taking a long swig. Carly finished up our drinks and handed one to me, which I accepted gratefully before taking a slow sip. Carly made the best drinks.

"What will Peter have, Desi?"

I froze, trying to think. I really had no idea what his drink of choice was. I supposed that's just how it was when you are still getting to know someone. "Oh, er. I'll bring him a beer, I think."

For some reason, this small hesitation brings Benji back into my head and I stole a glance to where he and Kira have settled themselves on Carly's sofa. They were talking animatedly, one of her hands rested companionably on his knee as she threw her head back laughing at something he'd said. He was laughing too, his eyes crinkled and his grin as wide as I've ever seen it.

"Benji likes rum," I said absently.

"Oh! I've got just the thing for him then!" Carly responded even though I hadn't really meant for her to hear it.

She finished up and handed me the beer for Peter and we walked back to join the others. Me sipping my gin as I tried to turn my attention to Peter instead of Benji and Kira.

"Hey! Look who's back to rescue me," Peter teased as he pulled me to his side, wrapping an arm around my shoulder.

"I wasn't sure what your drink of choice was, so I brought you one of Liam's beers." I smiled up at him as I handed over the bottle. He smiled and took a drink.

"That's sweet, thanks, Desi. Though for future reference, I'm a vodka guy."

I heard Carly behind me talking animatedly to Benji as she gave him his drink. Explaining something about the origins of the rum. "Ah, thanks! I'll have to buy a bottle of this." I heard his Scottish lilt and my chest tightened.

"Desi said you liked rum, so I knew you'd love this."

"She did, did she?" I don't turn around, but I swore I could feel his hazel gaze on the back of my neck and my skin prickled at the thought.

"I was just telling your friends here about the new project we've been working on at the office, Desi." Peter's voice broke into my thoughts as I returned my attention to the group.

"Oh, um, right." My eyes flickered between my friends who stood across from me. Both raising their eyebrows, seemingly amused by something. "It will be huge for the firm, and our careers!"

"I've heard of Ball-Barlow. It's very impressive that you've landed their business," Meredith said matter-of-factly, "I've also heard their CEO is quite attractive... and single." She smirked, and Eliza fanned herself dramatically.

"*Quite attractive* is the understatement of the century, Meredith," Eliza said. "The man is smoking hot. He was on New York's list of the sexiest men alive last year. Do you think you'll get to meet him for the project?"

I shrugged. "I'm not sure. Every company operates a little differently. Some of the higher ups like to be hands on and others would rather delegate."

"I'd like to get my hands on him." Eliza bit her lip suggestively and I giggled.

"And what would Harvey think of that?"

Eliza laughed and slapped my arm teasingly. "Ah, come on now, Desi. You know that man has absolutely nothing to worry about with me." She paused. "On the other hand, he absolutely needs to get his new shop set up and running so I don't have to spend so many nights alone... if you know what I mean."

I smirked. "Are you saying you are currently sexually frustrated, Liza?"

Peter choked on his beer next to me, covering his mouth with his forearm to catch the spittle. "This is that kind of friendship then?" He recovered himself enough to laugh fully. "I guess I'll have to keep that in mind for the future."

I patted him heartily on the back and for the first time this evening remembered why I liked him so much. This easy back and forth between us is what had first started those flutters in my stomach nearly a year ago. I gripped his shoulder firmly and raised up on tiptoes to brush a kiss on his cheek. I caught sight of Benji and Kira out of the corner of my eye when I did. They were still cozy on the loveseat. Benji's gaze met mine for a moment, and I quickly looked away.

"Don't worry, I don't kiss and tell, babe," I assured him.

"She's telling the truth, Peter. It's incredibly annoying." Eliza folded her arms and pouted. "She gets all the goods from me."

"Hey, now. It's not my fault you are basically an open book. I don't force you to tell me this stuff."

She broke her faux pout and nodded. "I guess you're right. A little reciprocation would still be appreciated, though."

"Anyway... back to the subject that was not Eliza's non-existent sex life..." Meredith cut in.

"Ah, yes. The Ball-Barlow CEO. What's his name again, Desi?" Peter asked, reaching out to grab my hand, holding it firmly, his skin warm against my own as he brushed his thumb intimately along the inside of my wrist. The simple gesture sent a zing of excitement down my spine.

"Peter. Don't tell me you haven't been doing your homework," I teased him. "Lincoln Nguyen is his name."

"You definitely have to fill us in if you get to meet the illustrious Mr. Nguyen, Desi. I'm dying to know what he's like in person," Meredith said.

I nodded. "Of course. We should know more about who exactly we will be meeting with next week. You'll be the first one I call."

Meredith snorted at the absurdity of this. "Point taken. And I need a refill. Anyone else?"

She and Eliza disappeared into the other room to refresh their beverages, and I was left standing alone with Peter. The sudden absence of my friends reacquainting me with the awkwardness of being with my new boyfriend in such close proximity to Benji.

"So, am I making a good first impression?" Peter asked, raising my hand to his mouth to plant a soft kiss against my knuckles. His steely gaze was earnest as he met my eyes.

"Absolutely." I smiled. This was the truth. Both Meredith and Eliza were tough cookies to crack, but he had clearly already charmed them both. They weren't even pretending to give him a hard time anymore. "With those two anyway. And they are usually the difficult ones."

Carly sidled up beside me, bumped her hip playfully against mine, and wrapped an arm around my waist.

"So, Peter, you've got quite the catch here if I do say so myself." She smiled at him. "It's honestly so great to finally meet you. Thank goodness you finally got the hint and took this lady off the market. Just in time too!"

I stiffened as Carly continued talking. Hoping Peter didn't catch the "just in time" bit or if he did, he would just brush it off as light teasing. I knew what Carly meant by it. "Just in time" before Benji re-entered my life. I really didn't want to have that kind of conversation with Peter so early in our relationship.

I zoned out a bit as the two of them continued talking. Kira's laugh tittered in the background as I tried not to think about the pair of them sitting together. I had no real right to be upset if they were hitting it off. Even if I had hoped that my past with Benji was enough of a reason for her to put him in the "do not touch" category. He wasn't mine.

I caught the tail end of Carly and Peter's conversation as I heard Peter excuse himself to the bathroom.

Carly turned to me as he walked away, hand on her heart and a grin on her face. "Seriously, Desi. He's great." I tried to smile, but I could hear Benji's voice behind me and it didn't quite reach my eyes.

Carly's expression changed immediately. She may not be the most brilliant intellectual among my friends, but she was always the most insightful when it came to reading other people. Especially people she cared about. Eliza had referred to her as an empath on more than one occasion.

"Oh, sugar. What is it?" she asked with concern in her eyes.

I stole a glance over my shoulder at Benji and Kira, both so into whatever they are talking about that they didn't notice. "It's nothing, Carls. Seriously. I'll be fine."

Carly's gaze had followed mine and even though I turned my attention back to her face, she was still watching the couple on the loveseat carefully, her eyes narrowed as she reached up to grip my shoulders.

"Desi, that boy over there is head over heels for you. If you want him, you should get him. Don't get me wrong; Peter is lovely too. But you are my friend, and I just want you to be happy." She whispered it, the whole while her gaze on Benji and Kira. She turned her face up to me finally, her gaze still serious. "Trust me, honey. I know people." She stood on her tiptoes to wrap me in a tight hug, patting my back gently.

"But... that's a problem for future Desi, either way. Let's get everyone together for a game! Truth or Dare? Never Have I Ever? Monopoly?" Back to her usual bubbly optimism, she led me to the living room, and we all settled into the sectional and chairs for a game of Never Have I Ever.

Somehow, I ended up being chosen to go first. I thought quietly for a moment, long enough for Benji to tease me with a "Nothing you haven't done, then?" and a wink which made Peter squeeze my knee tighter.

I rolled my eyes at the comment, but I couldn't look directly at him. He was cozied up to Kira, their thighs nestled against each other. Her hand rested on his leg while he leaned forward, his elbows on his knees and his hands folded in front of him.

"Never have I ever... made out with two people in one night." I grinned devilishly and eyed Kira, waiting for her to take her drink. Benji, Peter, Eliza, and Carly all drank as well.

Meredith, Liam, and I raised our own glasses together.

"To being prudes!" Meredith cheered and the three of us took a swig.

"Eliza, you next!" Carly said animatedly.

"Never have I ever had sex in a public place."

I took my drink and gave Peter a wink as I caught him eyeing me with new curiosity. Benji, Kira, Carly, and Liam all drank.

We went through a few more rounds of lighter topics before it came to Benji.

"Never have I ever set the kitchen on fire boiling rice." He grinned at me as I took my drink.

"Not fair. That was obviously aimed at me." But I smiled as I said it, the gin starting to make my head feel fuzzy. Peter had swapped to water since he was driving us home.

"It was quite an accomplishment, lass." He winked and then turned to Kira. "Your turn now it seems."

Kira tapped her finger to her lips while she considered. "Never have I ever slept with a coworker." She eyed me carefully, as Peter and I each took a drink. As well as Meredith, Carly, and Liam.

Benji sat up a bit straighter, but he didn't take a drink. He studied me so intensely that I had to look away, my cheeks flushed.

We went around a few more times, laughing and drinking before we abandoned the game altogether and switched to reminiscing and fab five history lessons for Peter. It ended up being a fantastic evening and by the end, whether from the gin or the laughter, I couldn't remember exactly why I was so uncomfortable in the beginning.

Peter and I said our goodbyes and were about to leave when I decided my bladder needed one last empty before the drive back. I waved off Meredith and Eliza, who slipped out the door on their way home, and left Peter to chat with Carly and Liam.

I turned the corner from the kitchen toward the hallway and that's when I saw it. Benji and Kira standing beside the window looking out at the view. Benji's arm around Kira's waist as he whispered in her ear and she flashed a sultry smile as she turned to lean against the wall, pulling Benji with her until they stood face to face.

You think you know exactly how you would feel when this sort of thing happens to you. I know I did. I grew up on romance movies and books and poetry and all those cliché "girly" sorts of things as my brother Cy would say. I had sobbed into my pillow at heartbreak on my TV screen or on the pages of a book, struggling to finish the page through the tears clouding my vision.

Real life was different though. It was simultaneously not as awful as I had imagined and worse than I could have ever dreamed.

I felt it now.

Kira leaned back against the wall and Benji stood in front of her, his hands resting on her hips as her arms wrapped around his neck, holding his face close to hers. Their breaths came quickly as their eyes locked and Benji's lips murmured something as Kira's mouth turned up in a small smile. It was so intimate that I almost felt like a voyeur witnessing it. I didn't want to watch. I should turn away.

But I couldn't. I was frozen in place, unable to move. Unable to breathe as my chest tightened and my throat burned.

I would have thought I'd be crying already, really. But my eyes were bone dry. Maybe it was shock?

A moment later their lips met, their eyes closing as Benji pulled Kira close to him, moving one hand around her lower back, the other traveling up to rest at her neck as their kiss deepened. My heart stopped. My chest so tight that I thought it had surely compressed my heart into a tiny, shriveled mass.

He softened the kiss, to pull away from her and his eyes opened. He saw me finally. Standing, watching, staring. He pulled away quickly, an unnatural movement considering the prior tenderness. This was enough to break my trance, and I turned away and entered the bathroom. It was where I'd been headed, after all. Benji didn't know how long I'd been standing there watching.

I closed the door and pressed the lock before leaning

back heavily against its firm expanse. Feeling better at the solidness of it between me and them.

The tightness in my chest eased a bit and suddenly my body doesn't seem to know what to make of this. My lungs heaved as though I'd been holding my breath and I sank to the floor, my face in my hands as the tears finally stung my eyes and I quieted my sobs into my fingers. The whole time feeling like an utter idiot.

This was stupid. I was being so stupid. He had every right to carry on with Kira if he wanted. She was a good person. She was beautiful and funny and smart. She was perfect for Benji, really. She was good for him. And she was my friend.

I got my tears under control and stood to splash a bit of cool water on my face and make sure I looked presentable enough in the mirror. My eyes were a bit puffy, my nose a tad swollen. Otherwise, I was no worse for wear after my mini-meltdown.

I did my business, washed my hands, and returned to Peter, more than ready to get out of here.

7

The next morning, I woke to a throbbing headache and the torturous sun blazing through the sheer curtains of my bedroom. I'd been too drunk to close the blackout curtains before passing out in bed last night. I whimpered and pulled a pillow over my tender eyes as I tried to gather my bearings to get out of bed.

The drive home had been awful. I got the spinnies almost immediately and spent most of the journey bent over with my head between my knees. Embarrassed beyond belief as Peter rubbed my back sympathetically with his free hand.

"I swear this is not a regular occurrence," I had moaned, pressing my fingers to the bridge of my nose in an attempt to keep the nausea at bay.

He had been gracious about it, with the back rubbing and all. I needed to call him today as soon as my head felt a little less like it might explode at the slightest sound.

I rolled out of my bed and crawled to where I had dropped my bag the night before, digging out a bottle of painkillers and popping three into my mouth before crawling back to the glass of water on my end table.

I considered myself mentally tough. It took quite a lot to get me to crumble. But hangovers were something I had never handled well. Maybe because I was also feeling stupid and beating myself up over it since it was my own fault that I felt so awful.

I climbed back under the covers and pulled the blanket over my face, trying to focus on my breathing... or anything other than how awful I felt. My head was pounding so badly that I was afraid I might be sick.

Just as I was beginning to feel human again, still drifting in and out of consciousness, a gentle tap echoed from the door. I lifted the blanket and peeked out from my dark sanctuary to find a freckled face and a pair of gold-hazel eyes peering through the crack. For a moment I considered pretending to be asleep. I couldn't deal with Benji and my confused feelings about him and Kira and a hangover all at once.

"Desi, I saw you lift the blanket. I know you aren't sleeping."

I groaned, but I didn't move.

"Can I come in, lass?"

I squeaked out a "sure" and I heard his footsteps as he came into the bedroom, shutting the door behind him. The bed shifted as he sat down on the corner. I risked another glance from under the blanket. He was not looking at me but rather at his hands folded between his knees. His forehead furrowed and he seemed conflicted about whatever he was thinking.

"About last night... I know..." he started, and I couldn't do this. I couldn't let him finish.

"It's no big deal, Benji. I'm happy for you guys." My voice

came out small and weak, cracking a bit on the word happy. I hoped he would write that off as my hangover and not this heaviness I was feeling in my chest at the memory of last night.

"Oh. Right. Well, good, I'm glad it's not an issue then. It's just... I saw you right after, you know, on your way to the loo. And your face... I just thought..." He inhaled sharply and let his breath out in a slow hiss. "I guess I misread the situation."

The painkillers had dulled the headache enough that the thought of another peek from my blanket haven didn't make me want to hurl. I lifted the blanket again, this time wrapping it over my head and leaving my face exposed. He still hadn't looked at me, his eyes on his hands as he rubbed his thumb over an open palm.

"Benji, I just want you to be happy. You know that. I'm glad you guys have hit it off." My chest tightened as I spoke, but my voice remained steady this time. He turned to look at me, a smile curving his lips before he took in my face wrapped in the blanket.

"Ah, shit, lass. You look like hell."

I gasped in shock. "Just what every girl wants to hear."

He laughed. "Sorry, I just didn't realize how badly you were feeling... do you want me to bring you some tea? That might help."

I nodded. "That sounds amazing, actually. Now that I don't feel like I'm going to puke at any second."

"Be right back, lass." He stood and strode out of the room. Back to the usual. Benji on a mission to get everything to rights.

Carefully I pulled myself out from under the blankets, fluffing my pillows and positioning them behind me so I could sit up comfortably. My head was now at a dull ache rather than a raging throb, but I still didn't feel like getting out of bed was an option. I closed my eyes, rubbing them with my fingers as they adjusted to the brighter light.

Benji returned with a steaming mug of black tea. He set it on my nightstand. "Tea for the lady. I hope it helps get you back on your feet." He turned to leave but paused for a moment in the doorway. "Peter seems like a nice lad. I'm glad you're happy, Desi."

"Thanks, Benji. He is. A nice guy, I mean." I smiled weakly at him, my heart constricting again as I looked at that familiar lopsided smile. Peter was a nice guy. He just wasn't Benji. I picked up the mug and held it up. "Thanks for this, too."

"Anytime, lass." He grinned and gave me a little salute before he disappeared down the hallway.

I sipped the tea and it was probably the best cup I've ever had. "Get it together, Desi," I whispered to myself. My head was in pieces, and it was not a feeling I was accustomed to or particularly fond of. "Get it together."

———

A FEW HOURS LATER, freshly showered, and with a belly full of toast, I called Peter. He didn't answer so I left him a message.

"Hi, it's Desi. I just wanted to apologize again about how out of hand I was last night. I'm sure that's not what you were hoping to get out of a fourth date. You were so nice about it, and I promise I'll make it up to you on date five. I mean... if there is a date five. I mean... shit. I hope I didn't completely blow things for us, and thanks again for being so understanding. Give me a call later or I'll see you at the office tomorrow. Talk soon."

I hung up and sighed. That was a disaster.

I checked my texts and saw that I had a few from Eliza and Carly. Mostly just gushing about how perfect Peter was and how happy they were to finally meet him. Apparently, he and Liam had really hit it off, talking baseball, and Carly wanted to set up a double date soon.

I was torn on how to feel. On one hand, Peter was great. Things had been going so well with him, and until a few weeks ago this would have been the best summer of my life. Benji was complicating things. He was getting in my head where I couldn't even enjoy this new relationship.

All this stuff with Benji was old news. These were teenager Desi problems, not adult Desi problems. Clearly, the issue was I had never gotten any resolution or closure from what had happened the last summer Benji had visited. I hadn't dealt with it properly. It had nothing to do with how I really felt about him now. At this point we barely knew each other, after all.

That was all this was. Just unresolved stuff from seven years ago. I just needed to figure out how to get it resolved so I could move on with Peter.

That's all it was.

8

BEFORE

I was fifteen the first time I looked at Benji in any sort of romantic light.

He had grown into his long limbs, finally. No longer the gawky and gangling pre-teen he had been the summer before. He still had maturing to do, obviously, but he was very unlike the ornery boy he had been and was showing signs of the man he would soon be. My own hormones had also struck in full force and the combination of our emerging sexualities had meant a summer full of awkward flirting and accidental touches.

That summer had ended with my first kiss. A boy down the block named Todd who was everything Benji wasn't. Serious, quiet, and very obviously interested in me. Where Benji had always left me feeling confused about where I stood and how he felt, Todd made it perfectly clear. So, despite my heart being set on the Scottish boy, I had turned my attention to the red-headed one.

Benji had pulled away in the face of my new "relationship", if you could call it that, and by the end of the summer it was like none of those early weeks had even happened. He

64

had departed back to Scotland with a friendly hug and a flash of that lopsided grin.

By the time school had started again, Todd and I were just a distant memory. Things fizzled fast at that age.

I still found myself thinking of the freckled Scottish boy all the way across the ocean. Looking back on this time in my life, I wrote off my infatuation as a girlish fantasy. He was away, he was unattainable and so he was fascinating.

My freshman year of high school had been filled with attention from older boys. I had dated a few of them briefly, but Eliza, Kira, and I had decided that we didn't want to get into any sort of serious relationship. We had each other. The boys were just some fun.

Two more summers of coy flirtation ensued with Benji. My confidence had grown, and I found myself enjoying his attention and company without the agonizing pining and wondering I had tortured myself with the summer I was fifteen. Our relationship eased back into the friendly banter it had been as kids, and I was able to mostly ignore the underlying heat and physical attraction. We were friends.

And then, the summer before my senior year of high school, things changed.

The awkward flirtation had returned. I found myself making excuses to spend time alone with him. So, when Kira's parents were away and she had masterminded a house party for all of us, I eagerly dragged Benji along with me.

I can remember that night so clearly. I thought of it often in the years since. It was late July, and it was hot. So hot that the short walk from my house to Kira's left us both panting and sweaty. We had crashed into the air-conditioned haven with relief and, laughing, made our way to the kitchen to find my friends.

"Desi! You made it!" Eliza hugged me. "Ew, and you're all sticky, gross." She held my shoulders and carefully pushed me away from her, her face twisted in disgust.

"It's just a little sweat, it's crazy hot out there." I went to the refrigerator and opened it to peek inside and enjoy the extra cold air. Benji sidled up behind me, peering over my shoulder.

"There's some beer in there, grab what you want!" Kira called from her seat at the kitchen island. A few other people were milling about, and she returned her attention to them, talking animatedly as usual.

My lips curved in a conspiratorial grin and I grabbed two bottles from the shelf. I closed the door and turned to face Benji, an eyebrow raised. "Want one?"

He smiled widely and took the bottle from my hand. "This is legal for me across the pond, you know. It's not nearly as much of a 'fun and dangerous rebellion' for me." He twisted off the cap and took a swig, making a sour face as he swallowed. "American beer is awful."

I opened my own bottle and took a sip, enjoying the ice-cold liquid on my tongue. It was refreshing, if not the best thing I had ever tasted. "Well, we can't all be as classy as you Europeans."

He snorted and then leaned back against the counter and this time his smile is soft as he studied me, taking another drink. "You don't strike me as the rebellious type, lass."

I huffed, offended. "What's that supposed to mean? You think I'm a goody-goody or something?" I crossed my arms across my chest.

His grin returned and he laughed. "No, not at all. This just doesn't really seem like your usual speed. Do you go out drinking often?"

I bit my lip and considered this. "Hmm... a few times." I tapped my finger against my cheek as I thought. "You're right, though, it's not usually what I'd prefer to be doing most of the time. This time it's different. This is Kira's house. She's my friend, and I'm comfortable here." I pumped my elbow against his arm. "And you're with me."

"Ah, yes. And my presence always makes everything more fun, aye?" He winked at me.

I laughed. "Well, I wouldn't go that far." I took another sip of my drink. "But I'm glad you're here."

I looked up at him and suddenly found it hard to breathe. He was standing so close, our arms brushing, and he met my gaze, his lips parted as though he was about to speak, and his expression was more serious than I'd seen it in a long time... maybe ever.

Just as I was about to open my mouth to break the intensity of the moment, Eliza came crashing into me. "Babe! You have to come dance with me! It's our song!" The familiar beat echoed from the living room.

I looked up at Benji again and he shrugged and smiled. "It's your song, lass. It's basically law that you have to go with her." I rolled my eyes at him. "I'll hold your beer, go." He took the bottle from my hands as Eliza pulled me into the living room.

The party had grown as Benji and I had enjoyed our drinks. The living room was packed full, and someone had turned on some sort of flashing lights. Eliza dragged me to the middle of the room and the two of us found our natural rhythm as we danced together, not caring that we bumped into other bodies every now and then. I lost myself in the moment, allowing all of my senses to be overwhelmed by the sound of the music and the movement of the others around me.

The song ended and, laughing and breathless, the two of us headed back to the kitchen. Benji leaned against the doorway to the living room, holding my beer, his gaze dark and almost smoldering. He handed me my bottle and followed us back into the other room as I took a swig.

"I'll be right back, Desi. I just need some water and then we are going right back out there." Eliza headed off to get her drink and I leaned against the wall in the kitchen, catching my breath. Benji stood across from me, unusually quiet.

"Cat got your tongue?" I teased.

He smiled. "That's one I haven't heard in a while."

"Or maybe ever..."

"I'm not usually at a loss for words, so you're probably right."

"Was my dancing that bad?" I asked.

He laughed finally and I relaxed the tension I hadn't realized I had been holding in my shoulders. "You are a great dancer, actually."

I held his gaze, feeling that same pressure in my chest as before from the force emanating off him. He stepped forward then, resting his palm against the wall over my shoulder as he leaned in close. I couldn't move, I could barely breathe. *This is Benji. It's just Benji.* I told myself but it didn't seem to matter to my racing heart.

"Want to dance with me, lass?" His breath on my face made me shiver.

"Well, I've got to... finish this." I held up the bottle of beer that had just a few swigs left. He took it from my hand and tossed back the rest before leaning to drop the bottle in the trash can.

"Anything else you need to do first?" He grinned at me and I smiled back.

"Not a single thing I can think of."

He took my hand and the brush of his fingers against my palm sent tingles down my spine. He led me back to the dark living room and the writhing mass of dancers. The beat was hypnotic and soon we found ourselves pressed close together, his hands on my hips and his gaze never leaving my face. The dancing did nothing to distract me from how his touch made me feel. I was hyper aware of exactly where each of his fingers pressed against me and without even thinking, I reached up and snaked my arms around his neck, pulling him closer.

He smiled and leaned down. "This is even better than watching you, lass."

His words tickled my ear and my breath caught in my chest. I stood on my tiptoes to whisper in his ear, "You haven't seen anything yet." And I turned my head and pressed my lips to his.

He stiffened for a moment. I'd taken him by surprise. But it was only a moment and then he returned the kiss enthusiastically. His hands tightened at my lower back as he pulled me even closer so that every inch of us was touching as we continued to move to the rhythm of the pounding music. When we finally pulled away, we were both panting. I grabbed his hand and pulled him away from the crowd, up the stairs, and into the guest bedroom.

"Desi, I'm sorry. I shouldn't have..." Benji started once the door had shut behind us. I pushed him back against the door and stopped his words with another kiss.

I pulled away for a moment. "Don't be sorry. Please don't be sorry. I'm not sorry."

He wrapped a hand around the back of my neck and brought my mouth back to his, kissing me slowly this time.

The urgency and the need were gone, but the intensity still remained.

I'd had boyfriends before. Gone on dates that had progressed past a simple kiss. I had several experiences where we had been "rounding third" in that ridiculous baseball analogy. But I had always put a stop to things before anyone got too close to home. I had never really felt the desire to take things that far with anyone else.

That night with Benji had been different. I had never felt such a need for someone. I kept kissing him like if I stopped, I might not be able to take another breath. He finally gave in and returned the desperate pace I was setting for us.

My hands shook as I reached for the buttons on his pants and he pulled back suddenly, grabbing my wrist as he looked down at me through lust-narrowed eyes.

"Are you sure?" He whispered the question, and I nodded in reply. Standing on my toes to plant kisses along his neck as he loosened his grip on my wrists and I returned to my original mission. In a moment his pants are undone, and my hand cupped the building hardness of him across the fabric of his boxer briefs. He hissed in response, and I smiled. I reached back to turn the lock on the door and then bent with the intention of going to my knees before him. Before I made it all the way down, he pulled me up by my elbows and instead walked me backwards until the backs of my knees bumped against the edge of the bed and I collapsed back on the mattress.

"Benji, what are you..." I started but he put a finger to my lips while his other hand slipped under my skirt flickering across the wetness of my underwear and my breath hitched in response.

"Lay back, Desi," he ordered, and I followed his instruction without hesitation.

In a moment, his head had dipped below my hemline, fingers pulling down the underwear in his way as his hot breath trailed kisses up my trembling thighs. I was shaking so hard now with anticipation that I brought my hand to my mouth and bit down in an attempt to quiet the trembles. His tongue tasted me hungrily and my back arched as I moaned against my palm, my free hand reaching down to curl against Benji's head, encouraging him. Not that he needed it. I could feel his own soft moans against me as he continued circling his tongue. His long fingers gripped my hips more firmly, pressing me back to the mattress as he slowed to a tortuously slow pace with his mouth.

"Benji. Please, I want you. Please."

He gave me one last long and teasing lick before he moved up to kiss me deeply, his erection pressing promisingly against my thigh through the thin layer of his underwear. "You're sure that's what you want?"

He pulled a condom out of the pocket of his pants that had been discarded on the floor and held it up.

"Yes, put it on," I answered, my voice now a low throaty moan.

He leaned over to kiss me deeply once more before he ripped open the package and rolled the condom on. He hooked his arm under my leg and pressed the tip of himself against me. The trembles started again as I ached to feel him, all of him. I pressed myself against him, easing the tip inside and he held me steady as he inhaled sharply.

"Oh, fuck." His gaze found mine, eyelids heavy, and he slowly slid in further. I groaned a bit, feeling slight discomfort at this unfamiliar sensation, but the desire I felt for him overrode the slight momentary physical pain. I nodded at him and he slid further in, filling me completely before pausing again. "You okay, lass?"

I pulled him down to kiss him and he shifted his weight heavily on top of me, removing his arm from under my knee. His tongue found mine desperately and he started to rock against me, the friction easing the discomfort as my body responded to the sensation. I moaned into his mouth. He reached up and pulled down the top of my tank, baring my breast, and used his thumb to circle my nipple. I pulled away with a hiss as the pleasure filled my belly. Moaning into his shoulder as his pace became more frantic. He moved his now free mouth down to my breast, licking and sucking as he drove into me faster, and I was moaning so loudly now that he brought a hand to my face, muffling my noises a bit. I responded by taking his finger into my mouth and drawing against it hard.

"Desi..." His whisper was thick with desire as he came, his pace slowing as he thrusted in and out at a leisurely pace before finishing motionless and satisfied on top of me.

Afterward we lay together in the bed, neither of us talking, but his fingers made slow and intimate circles on my bare shoulders. I leaned up and kissed him fully on the mouth once more before I started to get myself dressed.

"You're amazing, lass," he said suddenly, and I looked over my shoulder at him, grinning.

"Took you long enough to figure that out."

9

*T*he office was a madhouse this morning. We were getting ready for the final pitch for the Ball-Barlow project. As it turned out, CEO Lincoln Nguyen was very much the "hands on" type as he was to be in attendance. Unsurprising, given the huge growth the line of hotels had had since he had taken the reins from one of the aging founders, Vince Ball. I checked over my notes and the presentation one last time before I headed to the conference room to get everything set up.

Jillian sat at the large table. Her notes were strewn across the surface in front of her, along with the handouts she had prepared for our clients. She looked up as I entered and smiled.

"You ready for this?"

I set down the laptop on the table and plugged it into the projector to get the presentation ready and I nodded. "As ready as I'll ever be, I suppose."

"Don't worry," Jillian said, "You're going to kill it. I know how hard you've worked on this."

"Thank you, that means a lot." I smiled gratefully at her.

Peter strode into the room with Nathan from the marketing department following close behind. Things had been back to normal with Peter; he had been incredibly forgiving about my less-than-attractive drunkenness over the weekend.

Peter and Nathan took their seats at the table and chatted excitedly with Jillian. I couldn't bring myself to join into the chatter with the butterflies in my stomach acting up. I checked my watch. Five more minutes.

The elevator doors opened and Tom, our vice president, emerged with three others trailing behind him. One man, older and balding, was talking to Tom with enthusiasm, his hands moving frantically with his words. A woman, in her mid-forties it seemed, dressed in a simple but sophisticated black pantsuit followed them stoically. Finally, the last man brought up the rear, his cell phone in hand as he typed on the keyboard, obviously attempting to get out one last communication before our meeting.

He was tall, probably 6'3", and a solidly built man. I could see the outline of a trim waist under his suit jacket. He finished whatever he had been doing on his phone and clicked a button to shut it off before sliding it into his pocket.

I could get a good look at his face now, and Meredith had not exaggerated when gushing about Lincoln Nguyen. He was drop dead gorgeous. His high, prominent cheekbones and his well-defined jaw. His eyes were so dark they were nearly black, and they shone with such passion that I could practically see his drive and ambition working behind them in his brain. His full lips broke into a wide grin as he entered the room and leaned across the table to shake

Jillian's hand, greeting her warmly. He tossed a friendly wave to me, Peter, and Nathan before making his way down to the end of the table to his seat.

"Desi?" I heard Peter's voice and shook my head a bit to clear my thoughts. He was looking up at me, a smile on his face but his brow creased in concern. "You all right?"

I smiled. "Yeah, I'm great." The brightness in my voice sounds alien to me, and I took a drink from my water bottle and shuffled through my notes a final time.

Finally, Tom finished up the beginning of the pitch and turned to me. "I'll turn this over to our Junior Associate now, Desi Palmer. She's brilliant, and she's been working extremely hard on this presentation for the last few weeks." Tom smiled at me encouragingly, and I took a deep breath as I started the presentation, avoiding looking directly at Lincoln at the head of the table.

The presentation went smoothly and as I spoke, my confidence grew and the butterflies in my stomach settled to a low twitch. About mid-way through I met Lincoln's gaze, and he was studying me, the entirety of his attention on my face. I looked away and avoided looking at him for the rest of the meeting.

I finished my bit and took my seat next to Peter, who reached out under the table to squeeze my knee. "You did great, babe," he whispered, and the nervous energy drained from my body. Thank goodness this was over. I felt good about the presentation and my work. At this point all that was left to do was for the three people representing Ball-Barlow to decide if it was the best offer on the table. It was out of my hands.

WE WRAPPED up the pitch meeting and were exchanging after-meeting pleasantries when Lincoln looked down at the watch on his wrist. I had been impressed that he had not pulled his phone out of his pocket even once during the meeting. Many people in his position can't help themselves. Their ego drove their need to always be in contact.

"Well, it's about time for food. Any recommendations from the locals?" he asked.

Tom and Jillian both jumped in with suggestions. All fancy and expensive options that would require at least a twenty-minute drive further downtown. I pressed my lips together before I offered my suggestion.

"There's a new place just a few blocks from here that's fantastic. I know the head chef and can vouch for the quality." I smiled and met Lincoln's grateful gaze as he nodded.

"That sounds right up our alley. Care to join us?" He made the offer to the room, but his eyes didn't leave mine.

"I wish we could! We have another meeting across town we have to be at in an hour," Jillian apologized.

Tom countered, " Desi is free this afternoon! Maybe she can accompany you?"

I stiffened briefly but forced a smile to my face. "Absolutely, I'd be happy to."

The late June weather had not yet turned hot, so we decided that the restaurant was close enough to head on foot. I tried for a few minutes to make conversation with Nina, who was Ball-Barlow's Marketing Director. She was friendly enough, but she didn't seem interested in carrying on a conversation with me. Her phone was in her hands, and she was clearly catching up on emails as we walked.

Instead, I positioned myself on the outside of the group next to George, the balding Director of Finance of the company. George was an enthusiastic conversationalist, as I had noticed when he had been speaking with Tom earlier. His hands moved almost as fast as his mouth. But he was more interested in talking to Lincoln than to me, so I strolled quietly along beside them, getting lost in my head before the sound of my name caught my attention.

"What about you, Desi?" Lincoln asked.

"Er, I'm sorry, what was the question?"

Lincoln laughed, his eyes crinkling in his amusement. "Passing that pizza place a few blocks back got us talking about pizza. George here claims that Italian sausage is the most superior topping. I say it's got to be pepperoni. What about you, Desi?"

"Pineapple and ham, for sure," I answered matter-of-factly.

Both men gasped, and George actually clutched his hand to his chest as if he'd been wounded. "Blasphemy."

I smiled. "I get that a lot."

I looked up and realized we have almost made it to the restaurant, and I pointed. "Ah, there's where we are headed. Just in time. Judging by the topic of conversation, we are all ready to eat."

We were seated quickly and made haste in studying the menu. My stomach gurgled. I was starving. I ordered the lobster mac and cheese and sipped my water while we waited for the food.

George continued to dominate the conversation, but every few minutes I caught Lincoln's warm gaze across the table. Finally, as George took a moment to catch his breath and swig his drink, Lincoln directed another question at me.

"So, you know the head chef here?" he asked.

I nodded. "Yes, we grew up together, actually. Well, sort

of. He's from Scotland but our parents are old friends, so we spent quite a lot of time together in the summer as kids."

"Scotland? What's he doing so far away from home?" I noticed he was leaning across the table toward me. George had fallen uncharacteristically silent.

"This restaurant just opened a few weeks ago. The original is in London. His boss sent him to Boston to get it started up." The pride in my voice was unmistakable as I talked about Benji's accomplishment. It was impressive that he had gained the respect and trust of his boss so quickly. Opening a new location was a tremendous responsibility.

Our food arrived, and we all tucked into our meals hungrily. Nina still hadn't put her phone away, and I saw Lincoln glance at her in annoyance a few times. George had seemingly run out of things to talk about or was just more interested in inhaling his steak and potatoes. We fell into a companionable silence as we ate.

"The food is fantastic. Great suggestion, Desi," Lincoln said between bites of his turkey club. "This aioli is one of the best I've ever had."

"Any fan of my food is a friend to me, mate." Benji had appeared at our table, grinning as he held out a hand to greet Lincoln. "I heard we had some special guests today. Pleasure to meet you, Mr. Nguyen."

Lincoln swallowed his bite and gripped Benji's outstretched hand. "Your friend here had nothing but outstanding things to say about the restaurant and you. The food has admittedly lived up to the expectation she set." He returned Benji's smile.

Benji glanced sideways at me, his expression curious, "Oh, she did, did she? I guess you'd rather compliment me behind my back then, lass?"

My face flushed. "Can't have you getting a big head, can

I? You do that well enough on your own, Ben." I winked at him, and my eyes trailed down to meet Lincoln's intense gaze across the table. Both men were studying me, and I struggled not to squirm under their stares.

Benji's eyebrow raised as he took in the expression of discomfort on my face and returned his attention to Lincoln, allowing me to relax back into my seat. "I'm glad you came by. Desi's great taste runs far deeper than food, as I'm sure you learned this morning."

Lincoln's eyes widened a bit at this, but he nodded his head slowly. "Yes, her presentation this morning has given us a lot to think about. We have been with the same design firm for ten years so it will take something outstanding for us to switch."

Benji nodded. "I am biased, but outstanding is Desi's middle name." He smiled again but it had lost its usual mischief, instead his expression was contemplative. "Anyway, I'll leave you all to your food now; just wanted to stop by and make sure things were going well and say hello. Enjoy the rest of your meal." He dipped his head, winked at me, and strolled back to the kitchen, leaving a void of silence in his wake.

"I can see why they sent him all this way to open this place," Lincoln said after another bite of his sandwich. "He can definitely hold his own."

"That's Benji." I smiled, and we finished our lunch with no further excitement. I steered the conversation discreetly back to the presentation a few times and though Lincoln was courteous, he gave nothing away during the rest of the meal. I supposed I would just have to be patient. These corporate jobs were never straightforward, after all.

I said my goodbyes outside the restaurant as their car arrived to pick them up and then, rather than heading straight back to the office, I turned and reentered the restaurant. I nodded to the hostess, pointing to the kitchen, and she waved me past. This wasn't the first time I'd dropped in on Benji at work.

I pushed past the swinging doors and found Benji at the counter kneading dough. I flung my arms around his waist, hugging him tightly. He stiffened under my touch before he cast his gaze over his shoulder and saw who had disrupted his careful, quiet job. "You scared the shit out of me lass." He laughed, his hands never slowing in their work.

"Thank you," I said into his shoulder.

"Aye, nothing to thank me for. I should be thanking you for putting our name out there to someone with as many connections as Lincoln Nguyen. You are really the one who did me a favor," he replied.

I scoffed. "Sure, sure. Whatever you say, Mr. Modest. Your food is amazing, and you know it."

He grinned at this, abandoning the dough for a moment as he faced me. My hands rested on the countertops on either side of his hips, and I realized how close we were and took a step back, crossing my arms across my chest as my heart started fluttering faster.

"Having amazing food means nothing if you don't have bodies coming through the door to eat it, Desi." He reached up and tapped a finger on my nose, his eyes crinkling in amusement, "So again, thank you. I appreciate your support."

"You're welcome. I've got to head back now, but you're still game for poker night, tonight?" I asked.

"Wouldn't miss it for the world, lass. See you tonight," he replied with a smile and then he returned to the dough. I slipped out of the restaurant and began my walk back to the office, my head spinning and my heart still beating wildly in my chest. It was so senseless, getting so worked up from just being physically near him.

Halfway through my walk back to the office, I caught sight of myself in a window and saw the smudge of flour on my nose. I grumbled as I dusted it off. He was going to pay for that later.

10

Our twice-a-month poker nights had been an ongoing event since freshman year of college. It was how the fab five had originated.

Eliza, Kira, and I had grown up together but after high school our lives had diverged. Eliza dived into cosmetology school, Kira had chosen Boston College for their business program, and I had gone to Suffolk University for design.

Meredith and I had been paired together as roommates while Carly had been a fixture in all my design classes. I was the glue between the five of us. We were all so different, but somehow, we complemented one another. We had disagreements occasionally, but at the end of the day we had each other's backs.

Slowly the poker, drinking, and expressly "girls only" nights had expanded to include Eliza's boyfriend Harvey and Carly's boyfriend Liam. This then evolved into the two boys, Meredith, and me playing a rather serious and competitive poker game while Kira, Carly, and Eliza cashed out early and turned to girl talk and drinking games.

Tonight was no different except there was a fifth face still lingering at the poker table, his amber eyes shining over the top of his cards.

"You're full of crap, lass," he teased me.

"You don't know that, or you'd have put me all in already." I grinned and returned my cards to the table, covering them protectively with my hands.

"Maybe I'm just not ready to put you out of your misery yet," he retorted. "Besides, you are definitely bluffing; your nose gets all crinkly when you've got a good hand. No crinkles in sight."

Liam, Meredith, and Harvey had all folded after a few rounds of bets through the turn. On the table lay the ten of hearts, two of hearts, jack of clubs, and king of diamonds.

Meredith, ever the expert in reading people, eyed me thoughtfully. "I don't know, Benji. She usually bets more aggressively when she's got a good hand, and she's already got this pot too rich for our blood."

Benji tossed in his remaining chips. "Well, I'm all in now. Let's see it, then."

He flipped over his cards: the ace of spades and queen of diamonds. Shit, he had a straight. I peeked at my cards again. Ace and king of hearts. There was still one more card to play.

I pushed in the rest of my chips and turned my cards over and Benji grinned. "Really riding on this last card, aye?"

"Just turn it over, Meredith."

A sly smile on her face, she picked up the card from the top of the deck and held it in front of her face, her grin growing wider.

"And... it's... the queen of hearts!" she cried out and flung the card on the table while I hooted in victory. My flush beat Benji's straight.

"Well played, Desi, well played," Benji said, his smile thoughtful as he watched me gathering my winnings. "Thwarted by the queen of hearts... how fitting."

I met his gaze and felt that familiar tightening in my chest. Dammit, that feeling needed to leave me alone. Our eyes locked and his smile softened further. "Well done, lass. Fair and square."

Before I could reply, Kira sidled up behind him, wrapping her arms around his neck and pressing a kiss to his temple. "How's it going over here, babe?" she asked, eying the chaos on the table.

Babe. My breath caught on the word even as Benji's eyes remained fixed on me. I forced myself to look away. Hopefully he hadn't seen my thoughts written on my face. "Oh, I just cleaned Benji out this round, Kira. You might have to pick up the next dinner bill."

She laughed. "Oh, Desi, you never change. Always with that competitive spirit."

I looked up at her sharply, the mocking tone of her voice taking me by surprise, but she wasn't looking at me. She had settled herself on Benji's lap.

"Now that the boring, serious, poker game is over, who is up for some drinking games?" she asked.

A chorus of agreement rang out across the room, and everyone migrated to the table as the boys worked to clean up the poker game.

"So, where's Peter tonight?" Liam asked as he gathered the cards, slipping them neatly back into their box while Harvey took care of the chips and Carly passed out fresh drinks to everyone.

"He had to work late on a different project so he couldn't make it," I replied, sipping my refreshed gin and tonic. "We are definitely both up for that Red Sox game double date soon, though."

"Awesome! He seems like a cool dude." Liam elbowed Harvey. "You'd like him."

Harvey grunted and nodded, his attention still on his task of clearing up the poker chips.

"How's Peter after your meeting with Mr. Tall, Dark and Serious?" Benji interjected and my face twisted in confusion.

"What do you mean?" I asked.

"The bloke you were having lunch with today," he replied.

I laughed. "Benji, those were clients, remember? Peter was there when I was volunteered by my boss to show them a nice time." I smiled and tilted my head at him, questioning. Where was he going with this?

"Well, he must have not taken a good look at how that man was looking at you."

"Benji. It was work. Lincoln Nguyen is the CEO of a multimillion-dollar company. His interest in me is purely professional."

"Oh my gosh! Desi! So he *did* come to the presentation?" Eliza gushed.

Meredith leaned forward and sighed, her chin in her hand. "Was he even more beautiful in person?"

"I didn't notice," I lied, my shoulders stiffening at this turn in conversation.

Kira eyed me from across the table where she was still perched comfortably across Benji's lap. "Oh, come on, Desi. No one is going to question your professionalism for simply noticing someone is objectively attractive."

I shrugged. "I mean, he was nice enough to look at, but I

am with Peter and he is so far out of my league that I never considered him that way."

"I'm telling you guys. Mr. Nguyen was massively into your friend Desi here," Benji said again, gesturing toward me. I scowled at him, eyes blazing. "He was practically drooling while he watched her from across the table." Benji laughed, and Kira squeezed his shoulder reassuringly.

"What's with the third degree here? I was doing my job. I didn't notice anything in his behavior indicating he was interested in me. End of story."

"You never do notice the obvious, Desi. I'm actually shocked you are so good at your job with such a blind spot in your attention to certain details," Kira shot back, and I was completely lost for words.

What the fuck was this about?

"What is your problem, Kira? I don't have to agree with your boyfriend's assessment of the situation, and you weren't even there."

"I've seen it for myself often enough."

I couldn't even begin to process what is happening or why. I pushed my chair back from the table and stood. All eyes were on me, and the others around the table seem just as stunned as I felt. "Right, well. I don't know what problem the two of you seem to have with me, but I'm not going to sit here and argue with you anymore. I need some air."

I retreated to the terrace. The door shut sharply behind me, and I sank into a chair, my face in my hands. My brain was so focused on trying to understand what had just happened inside that I barely registered the sound of the door opening and someone joined me on the terrace.

"I'll be fine, Carly. Just give me a minute and I'll come back in."

"Well, lass, thanks for the compliment, but Carly's a bit prettier than me."

I groaned. "Can you just give me a minute, Benji? I just need to clear my head after that."

He sat down in the other chair, quiet for a moment. "I'm sorry, Desi. I shouldn't have done that." I peered at him over the tops of my fingers, my eyes still narrowed in annoyance.

He continued, "For the record, it's true, but I didn't have to bring it up in front of everyone like that and put you on the spot." He paused for a beat. "Kira was out of line and I told her so. She's still a little worked up, though. You know how she gets."

I nodded. Kira and I had been friends for most of my life. She was a great ally, but she had a hell of a temper when someone was on her bad side. I guessed I was on her bad side now.

"Well, I honestly didn't notice it at lunch. Scout's honor." I sat back and dropped my hands from my face. "But do you know what I did notice? Flour. All over my nose." I leaned forward and gave him a playful punch to the shoulder. "And this one is for being such an ass tonight." I jabbed him once more, and he reached up to grasp his shoulder in mock pain as I sank back to my chair.

He grinned brightly for a moment before his face fell once more into a serious expression. "So, are we good?"

I nodded. "Yeah, we're good."

He stood and held out a hand to me. I took it and he pulled me to my feet, a little more forcefully than I expected, and I found myself pressed against him, my arms around his neck as I tried to steady myself. The second time today we had been so close, and it sent my heart going once again.

My face flushed pink and I cleared my throat as I took a step back, finding my feet again.

"Sorry. Clearly, I learned to walk yesterday."

"We've been closer than that before, lass. Not a worry." He smiled, but it looked like he was affected by the sudden physical closeness as well. "Let's get back inside, then? I think Carly will move the party out here if we don't."

"Yeah, let's go inside. There is definitely not enough room out here all of us."

11

---

*L*ater that week, Eliza and I were making dinner at the apartment she shared with Harvey. He was out late again, working on the tattoo parlor he was opening in the next few months. It was temporary, but Eliza wasn't used to spending so much time alone, and the rest of us were trying hard to make sure she wasn't feeling too lonely during this transition.

We decided to do a movie night with homemade pizzas, and we were buzzing around her tiny kitchen getting all our ingredients together and just catching up.

"So, your big presentation went well, then? I feel like I haven't seen you in ages." She pouted a bit at this, and I laughed and pressed her close in an affectionate side hug.

"It did go well. We haven't heard back yet, but I'm feeling confident about it. The CEO seemed quite receptive," I said, but my face darkened a bit at the mention of Lincoln Nguyen. Eliza noticed my changed expression and raised an eyebrow at me.

"Ah, yes. Receptive." I flashed her a dark look and her face just twisted into amusement. "I didn't want to get in the middle of it the other night, but Benji and Kira aren't really wrong. You aren't the best at determining when someone is into you."

I rolled my eyes. "Maybe so, but there is a time and a place to discuss my personal shortcomings. And a way to do it without putting me on the spot like that. They were both way out of line the other night."

"I can agree with you there," she said as she sprinkled a handful of black olives over the cheese on her pizza. "But you know how Kira is when she gets her panties in a twist about something."

"It seems she's gotten good at deciding when to twist Benji's panties as well." I tried to say this in a light-hearted way but Eliza, ever perceptive, heard the edge in my voice.

"Moving on. How are things with Peter? I was hoping he'd make it to poker night so I could see how he and Harvey got along. Who knows when he'll be able to make it by again?" She sulked a bit at this, and I patted her arm sympathetically.

"He'll get the shop open soon and things will go back to normal, babe." I smiled at her, and she returned with a weak smile of her own. I hoped it was the truth. This situation was clearing wearing on her.

She flicked her pink tipped platinum hair over her shoulder. "We'll get through it. Anyway, Peter? How are things? I'm guessing he didn't notice anything amiss with you and Mr. Nguyen?"

I laughed. "No, Peter knows Mr. Nguyen is a client. Things are going well. We've both been so swamped these past few weeks that we haven't been able to spend much time together, but we have plans for tomorrow night. Something simple; he's going to come by and I'm going to make him dinner and we are just going to do the low-key night-in thing."

"Ah, I think I know what that means." She winked at me, and I scoffed.

"Is sex all you think about?" I asked, and her face turned to a pout again.

"You know how I get when I'm not having enough sex, Desi." She sighed. "This shop had better be worth it."

"It will be. You'll see," I reassured her again. "Anyway, no. This is not a night-in date to segue into sex. We aren't there yet." I avoided her gaze, and Eliza raised an eyebrow at me.

"Desi, you know I love you," she started. "Peter is a great guy... but do you think maybe you are only with him because you aren't afraid of losing him?"

I cocked my head at her as I arranged my pineapple slices across the top of my pizza. "What do you mean?"

"I mean being with him is safe. Because if it doesn't work out with him, you haven't lost much. Losing him wouldn't devastate you." She paused, studying me. "You two just don't seem to have that... 'spark'. Or at least, not kind of chemistry that you'd burn the world down for. Am I wrong?"

She popped our completed pizzas into the oven. I contemplated this for a moment before I shook my head. "What's so bad about that? What's wrong with protecting myself a little? What's wrong with taking things slow and growing into a relationship? Not everything has to be flames and fire, Liza."

Eliza placed a hand on my shoulder.

"There's nothing wrong with it, exactly," she said. "But anything worth having is worth risking. Don't you think?"

"Eliza, stop speaking in riddles and just spit it out. What is your point?" I asked with a sigh.

"Babe. Be real. Benji is who you want. You've been

pining for him for years, even if you don't want to admit it. And you are terrified. It terrifies you that if you let yourself feel those big feelings for him that you'll end up hurt again. Or end up hurting him. And losing him."

"He's with Kira, anyway. There's not much I can do about–"

Eliza cut me off. "Girl. I've seen the way he looks at you. Kira is not competition. I love her, but she's not right for him."

"And I am?" I asked.

"You're right for each other," she replied plainly. "And anything worth having is worth risking. You'll never forgive yourself if you don't risk this."

THE NEXT EVENING Peter arrived just as I was pulling dinner from the oven. I had decided on parmesan and herb crusted salmon with roasted asparagus and garlicky couscous. A simple meal that always looked and tasted more impressive than it was.

Peter settled himself on a barstool at the island with a glass of wine while I plated our food.

"Where are all of your roommates this evening?" he asked as he sipped the wine.

"My parents are at some work function for my mom. She works for a big accounting firm and they have 'customer appreciation' events." I paused my plating to emphasize this with air quotes. "Every few months. Really, I think they are all just so bored out of their minds running numbers every day that they just want an excuse to get drunk and cut loose."

Peter laughed. "Who could blame them?"

"Right?" I responded with a grin. "Luckily I'm not responsible for getting them home safely tonight. Benji kindly volunteered for that duty this evening."

I turned with a plate in each hand and moved to join him at the island. I may have imagined it, but I swore I saw him tense at the mention of Benji's name. I slid a plate in front of him and poured myself a glass of the wine.

He leaned over his food and inhaled deeply. "It smells amazing."

He reached over, a hand resting on my lower back as he pressed a gentle kiss to my temple. I closed my eyes, willing myself to give into his touch. To feel something like what we had in the beginning.

"Dig in," I said and popped a piece of asparagus into my mouth.

"Don't need to tell me twice."

We ate in companionable silence for a few minutes before falling into casual conversation about our various work projects and life in general. We hadn't spent much time together lately outside of work meetings, so it was nice to catch up.

After eating I tidied the kitchen, and the two of us found ourselves nestled together on the sofa with refreshed glasses of wine in our hands.

We had ended up here under the premise that we would find a movie to watch but instead we were simply enjoying conversation and neither of us had so much as attempted to find the remote control or turn on the television.

Finally, Peter suggested we play a game instead.

"Would you rather?" he suggested and with a low groan I agreed.

"You're as bad as Carly wanting to play these party games!" I teased.

"You start," he said with a smirk.

"Hm... okay. Would you rather..." I tapped my finger against my lips as I considered. "Be fired from your job or have your car repossessed?"

"Oh, the car. Definitely the car," he responded with zero hesitation.

I gasped. "But your credit score!"

He shrugged, his smirk widening, "Can be rebuilt! Being fired will follow you around for your entire career."

"Sure, unless you plan to work for yourself. As my own future employer, I'm not concerned about my employment record."

"But your credit score on the other hand... that might be a deal breaker for hiring yourself?" His eyes flash with good humor and I throw my head back in laughter.

"I'm a tough boss, what can I say?" I shot back and then playfully elbowed him in the arm. "Your turn."

His own laughter quieted, and his expression softened into something more thoughtful and serious. His steely gaze met mine and my heart constricted in my chest. I was not exactly sure what was coming but the shift in the energy between us was palpable.

"Would you rather be with me or with Benji?"

His eyes remained caught on mine as the air left my lungs. My eyes widened and just before I could force myself to reply, a reassurance to him, he let out a sigh and looked away.

"My timing is the worst," he said, and I reached out to grab his hand. He let me take it, interlacing our fingers easily. Our hands fit together so naturally. *We* fit together so naturally. So why wasn't this easier? I squeezed his hand, and he returned his gaze to my face, a sad smile on his lips.

I put my free hand against his cheek and leaned in to

kiss him tenderly. He raised his own hand to my jaw, cupping my face gently and running his thumb over my cheek.

I pulled away and whispered, "I'm so sorry, Peter."

"I know." He smiled sadly again. "I should've asked you out months ago. I'm kicking myself for blowing this by waiting so long. Though... I guess maybe it's for the best. If we'd had more time it just would have hurt worse when you chose him." He leaned back to move away from me then and released my hands to rub at his eyes. "Shit. I'm sorry."

He stood, and I let him.

"I know it's a cliché, but I do hope we can still be friends at some point," I said, my throat felt thick, and my stomach twisted. I had truly liked Peter. Life certainly had a twisted sense of humor throwing Benji back into my world just as I was finally moving forward.

He nodded and moved to leave. "I hope so too, Desi Palmer."

The door swung shut behind him, and I was left with my thoughts just as scrambled and confused as before.

"Goodbye, Peter Grayson," I whispered into the empty room.

12

Things hadn't been quite the same for me and Kira since poker night. In fact, we hadn't spoken at all since. That had been over two weeks ago now. I'd expected her to call or text within a few days to apologize. She was a lot of things, but Kira was normally willing to accept and own up to her mistakes. She would have apologized by now if she'd had any inkling she had been in the wrong.

I'd heard nothing.

Asking Benji about it wouldn't help matters so I simply didn't talk to him about Kira. I didn't want to make things awkward for him since they were seeing each other, even if it was still new and casual. Even if they were a terrible pairing. Even if he should be with me.

So, when Carly invited me to her 4th of July party, I hesitated. I knew Benji would be there with Kira. I hadn't seen the two of them together since poker night and not since I had ended things with Peter. The breakup had been the right thing to do. It wasn't as if I was expecting to just fall into Benji's arms afterwards. He had his own life. I had no right to toss a grenade in by confessing my feelings when he was dating someone else.

Eliza said I was being an idiot, and maybe she was right. But when I thought about telling him how I felt... it felt wrong. It felt icky and underhanded. Even if Kira and I were on the outs, it felt like disloyalty to make a move on Benji while they were together. Especially since I was still very confused about how I was feeling.

In the end, Carly wore me down and I agreed to come. At least I'd have Eliza, Carly, and Meredith there. They'd be good buffers between me and Kira if things got awkward.

Then, a few days before the party, they started dropping like flies. Harvey surprised Eliza with a trip to New York City. I was happy for her as I knew that the preparation for opening his shop had been hard on her and their relationship. Meredith ended up having to cancel due to a last-minute change in the case she was working. She'd be pulling all-nighters prepping briefs and other documents so they would be ready in time for the court hearing.

That left Carly.

I loved that woman to death, but she could be so clueless sometimes. That fact, combined with her playing hostess at this party, meant things were bound to get weird. I was considering backing out myself when Benji bought it up at dinner one night.

"So, you will be at this party tomorrow, right?" he asked casually.

I was caught off guard. I hadn't even decided for sure *not* to go and so I didn't have an excuse handy. *Damn it.*

"Uh, yeah, I guess I am. Carly would be disappointed if I didn't make an appearance, especially with Eliza and Meredith missing out," I replied.

It would have been so much easier to skip it and make

up an excuse later. Now I had two people counting on my attendance, and my resolve to bail on the evening weakened.

"Maybe we can catch a ride into the city together? Kira is working late and is planning to just meet me there."

My heart squeezed at the mention of Kira, but I nodded and replied brightly, "Sure, that would be great."

I got ready for the party with only one person on my mind. Benji.

I put on the shimmery golden dress and the complementary strappy sandals I had chosen for the evening and I thought of him. Would he like this outfit on me? Would he appreciate how the dress clung to my hips and accentuated my legs? Would he notice the care I took in painstakingly applying my eye makeup, the dark eyeshadow making my eyes glow an even richer hue of red-brown? Or how the black cat-eye curve of my eyeliner brought further attention to my long lashes? That I chose this perfume because he had commented on that particular scent more than a few times since he'd been here this summer?

Would he realize it was for him?

I felt like an idiot when the drive into the city yielded nothing more than the usual easy banter. Not even a single lingering look from him to give me any reason to think he was thinking about me in any way other than "just Desi".

I felt like an idiot when we walked through the door and Kira immediately wrapped herself around him, pointedly ignoring me as Carly squealed from across the room and scurried to my side. Benji was dragged into the living room and onto the sofa next to his girlfriend.

"You look, ah-mazing, Desi! Gold is totally your color. You should wear it more often. And you have got to show me how you did that smoky eye, girl!" Carly gushed over my appearance which made me feel even more stupid. I took a wine glass from the kitchen counter and poured myself an enormous glass of pinot grigio while Carly chattered on about the party and the other guests, none of whom I knew. They were all Liam's work friends.

"Later we can go out on the terrace and watch the fireworks! We've a great view of the displays near the bay," Carly continued before she spotted someone across the room. "Oh shoot, I've got to go introduce Gia to Lyle. Liam is sure that they'd get on really well." She gave a small wave to Liam's cousin who had just walked in the door. "I'll be right back, Des." She hugged me and then moved across the room, leaving me alone at the kitchen barstool. I took swallow after swallow of my wine and quickly emptied the glass, only to fill it again with what remained in the bottle.

No one approached me. I assumed I gave off a pretty convincing "fuck off" vibe. I had perfected that unapproachable look ages ago, and it had saved me from quite a few unwelcome advances in the past. I knew Carly was hoping to set me up with at least one of the men here tonight.

I was beyond not interested. Was considering vowing to be single and alone forever. Was avoiding looking into the living room where I knew Benji and Kira were cuddled up together on the sofa, whispering sweet nothings. Was determined never to pick out an outfit with a man in mind ever again in my life. Was feeling like a complete and utter idiot for thinking he might have noticed or that he might still feel something for me. Was feeling so stupid for having listened to Eliza when she said we were meant to be.

I took the last swallow of the wine and risked a glance in his direction. He was laughing, and for a moment his gaze met mine and my heart lurched.

I couldn't do this. I couldn't be here.

His brow furrowed in concern as he stood and started moving across the room. Before he could make his way to where I was sitting, I'd already moved to the door. I made it into the hallway and to the stairwell. I was not going to stand awkwardly waiting for the elevator and risk someone from the party seeing my emotional escape. I tried to keep my pace calm, so it wasn't quite so obvious that I wanted to run. When I made it down the first flight of stairs, I leaned against the wall and pulled out my phone to call a cab. That's when I felt his fingers on my shoulder. The frantic thoughts, the buzz of the wine, and tightness in my chest had left my ears ringing and I hadn't heard his footsteps behind me.

"Desi? Are you alright?"

I couldn't look at him. I would not be the drunken, jealous, crying girl. I would not.

"Hey." His curled finger pressed firmly against my chin and I turned my head up, but my eyes were on his chest. I couldn't look him in the face.

"Desi, look at me."

"I can't. I can't, Benji," I whispered.

"Why not?"

"Because I'm not going to cry about this. I'm just not."

"What are you talking about, lass? Did someone upset you upstairs? I'll go have a word. I'll make it better."

I shook my head. My words were caught in the thickness in my throat that had grown through this simple show of concern from him. He'd make it better. For me.

"No, no... it's..." I risked a glance up at his face. "I can't watch you with her anymore."

"What are you on about? Did Kira do something?" His gold-flecked eyes were so beautiful and the worry on his face was going to break me.

"Not exactly..." I shouldn't do this to him. I shouldn't tell him how I've been feeling. It was selfish to do this to him.

"Just come out with it."

I pressed my lips together, closed my eyes, and whispered. "I can't watch you with her anymore, because..." I swallowed and gathered my courage. "Because it should be me."

His fingers tightened their grip on my shoulders. I heard his breath, which had been coming in regular patterns, catch in his chest. I couldn't open my eyes.

The silence stretched between us and just as I was about to muster the courage to glance up at him, his mouth was on mine. Hungry and passionate. His hands left my shoulders to wrap around my waist, and my arms found their way around his neck, pulling him closer, needing every part of my body to be touching him. I moaned against his mouth as he pressed himself against, forcing me back against the wall until my senses were filled with him and only him. He smelled like pine soap and spicy cologne. He tasted like rum and sunshine.

When he pulled away, we were both breathing heavily. He rested his forehead against mine, and I resisted the urge to pull him back to me again. My heart pounded in my chest and when I finally looked him directly in the eye, he was grinning, eyes slanted up and cheeks flushed red under his freckles.

"I think that may have been the best thing I've ever heard in my life, lass." He touched his nose to mine, the smile softening. "As much as I want to stand right here forever and keep kissing you, I think I need to have a conversation upstairs first. Let's call you a cab, yeah? You go home and lie down. I'll be round in an hour or so."

I tightened my grip on him, not ready to part so soon.

Not willing to let him go back to her, even if it was to set things straight. Even if it was so he could be free to come to me.

I nodded as tears sprang to my eyes. Even as I was mentally scolding myself for being such a cliché. "Yeah. Yeah, I guess that's what we should do."

He pressed his lips to mine once more, softly and gently. I fought against deepening the kiss; my spine tingled with the desire to wrap myself around him and lose myself to his touch.

"An hour, tops. I promise." He stepped away and turned to go back upstairs.

Tears slipped down my face as I turned my back to him and called a cab home.

It took the entire cab ride home for me to realize why I was crying. It was tears of relief. It was knowing that this feeling I've been fighting isn't silly or stupid. It was knowing that he wanted me too. Relief.

This realization brought another round of sobs as I collapsed onto my bed and clutched my pillow to my face. My brain wouldn't turn off as I cried in the darkness. Doubts began to work their way into my drunken thoughts.

This would still be complicated. There was the matter of Kira. The matter of Benji's days in Boston being numbered. The matter of potentially ending our friendship for good if this didn't work out in the end.

My phone dinged and I pulled myself together long enough to check the message. *"This didn't go as well as I'd hoped. Will be a little later."*

Benji's breakup wasn't going swimmingly. Wonderful. I had no messages from Kira, though, which meant he was leaving my name out of his list of reasons they shouldn't be together. Or she was just too angry to confront me about it.

This would be so messy. So messy and stressful. I had dropped a grenade into his life. This wasn't fair to him.

But I wanted him.

More than anything I've ever wanted in my life. I could still feel the ghost of his hands on my waist. The taste of him, his lips pressed so urgently against mine. It had gone past want. I needed him.

I don't know how long I lay alone in the dark. My body was so tired from the emotional toll and sobbing that I fell asleep. I woke to someone moving in bed next to me and the familiar scent of Benji's cologne.

He scooted up behind me, draping an arm across my hip and nuzzling his face in my neck, inhaling deeply as he did. I half-turned to bring my face to his and placed my hand against his cheek, damp from tears. He sniffled a bit as I brought my lips to his and kissed him softly. His grip on my hip became firmer as he kissed me back before pulling away and burying his face in my hair.

"I'm sorry," I whispered into the darkness.

"It's not your fault, lass. I just don't like hurting people. Especially people I care for."

His voice broke a little, and he clung to me tighter, his fresh tears fell across the back of my neck and this time I turned around to face him fully, wrapping my arms around him tightly as he cried into my shoulder.

We fell asleep tangled together in my bed.

13

$\mathcal{T}$he sun beat into my bedroom the next morning, and I reached for him as I woke. The other half of the bed was empty. Panic rose in my chest until I realized I could smell pancakes cooking.

My lips curved into a smile as I allowed myself to feel happy and hopeful. I stretched slowly before I rolled out of bed and padded downstairs.

He had music playing in the kitchen. A catchy hip-hop song that he had turned up just loud enough that he could move along with the beat without it waking me upstairs. My small smile transformed to a wide grin as I watched him dance around the kitchen cooking breakfast. I could get used to this.

He turned to grab the platter to add another completed pancake and caught sight of me watching.

"Good morning, lass." He grinned and his eyes slanted in that way that made me weak in the knees. "Hungry? I've got the coffee going too, unless you'd rather tea." He knew that I usually preferred coffee, but I'd also professed to love his tea more than anything else.

I just loved him more than anything else. The thought stops me in my tracks for a moment. I loved him.

"Coffee is fine; you're busy with the rest of breakfast." I poured a mug for myself and one for him, knowing by the time breakfast was ready for eating the coffee would be at a drinkable temperature. I sipped at mine immediately anyway, inhaling the scent and wincing every so often at the heat.

Benji laughed. "Not waiting for it to cool this morning, are we?"

I smiled and shook my head, settling myself into one of my kitchen barstools to wait for him. "What can I say? My timing and my patience are awful these days." I threw out the lighthearted joke and wondered if he had thought the same thing last night.

He flipped the last pancake onto the serving platter and brought it, along with butter and syrup, over to the counter. The playful smirk went from his face now as he set the food down and studied me. "I'm glad for that, actually."

"You are?" I looked up at him from the barstool as he reached out to circle my waist.

"So glad." And he pressed his mouth to mine, and I felt like I was floating. My hands longed to touch him but were otherwise occupied with my hot mug of coffee. He pulled away again and sat down on the barstool next to me, making quick work of serving up the pancakes to both of us.

"So, let's talk about how much you love me." The gleam returned to his eyes as he took a bite of his pancake and I relaxed beside him, glad things have gone back to the usual lighthearted joking I was so used to. I rolled my eyes, but there was a smile on my face as I took a bite of my pancake.

He was joking, but he was right. I did love him. I wasn't ready to say it out loud just yet.

WE SPENT the rest of the day together, enjoying each other's company. My parents had gone to Maine for the weekend to visit my aunt, so we had the entire house to ourselves and we took full advantage of this. Touching, kissing, and cuddling every chance we got, knowing that in a few days we wouldn't have the luxury of exploring this new part of our relationship unhindered by the prying eyes of others.

I was sure my dad would be thrilled with this turn of events. I wasn't worried about their disapproval, exactly. It was just nice not to have the added pressure of their presence.

After dinner at Frank's, Benji decided he wanted to make cupcakes, so we swung by the store to gather ingredients, our hands entwined the entire trip. Benji taking every chance he could to raise our tangled fingers to his lips to kiss my hand tenderly. I teased him about being so cheesy, but the gesture made my heart beat faster every time.

Benji started to work as soon as we got home, and I settled myself at the counter to watch and steal tastes of the cherry ganache and chocolate buttercream.

"You are incredibly unhelpful, lass," Benji chided with a grin as he caught me sneaking the buttercream for the third time. "At this rate there won't be any left for the cupcakes."

"You can always make more." I grinned back, licking the sweet mixture from my finger.

He pulled a plate with two cupcakes from the fridge where he'd placed them to cool. The rest were on the counter, but he was too impatient for us to eat the finished product to wait for all of them to reach room temperature. He expertly cored the center of the cakes with the piping tip and squeezed in the chocolate cherry filling. He topped each cake with the buttercream and for good measure grated a dark chocolate bar over the top. He set one cupcake in front of me and carefully studied his own for imperfections as I stuffed half of mine in my mouth, groaning in approval as the mixture of flavors hit my taste buds.

Benji raised an eyebrow. "Can't even take a moment to appreciate my artistry?"

"Your artistry is being appreciated in my mouth," I replied, pointing to my cheek and speaking around the large bite I was still chewing.

He laughed and moved closer to me, standing between my knees. I finally swallowed my bite as he set his cupcake on the counter behind me. His hands lowered to my hips. "I wanted you to appreciate with your eyes first, but I suppose I can handle this." He leaned forward, his face close to mine and if I just tilted my head our lips would meet. I met his gaze from under my lashes and then, without warning, I lifted the half-eaten cupcake and smeared the chocolate frosting across the lower half of his face.

He leaned back but didn't step away as I dissolved into girlish laughter. "Agh. Really, Desi?"

I was laughing so hard I couldn't answer. One of his hands snaked behind me, warm fingers pressed into my lower back under my shirt as he leaned over and, in a flash, wiped his chocolate covered face from the deep v of my shirt all the way to my jaw. I squealed in response. "Benji!"

He grinned at me, frosting still smeared over his freckles. "Oh no, what have I done? Let me help you with that." And he dipped his head again. This time mouth opened to lick and suck my skin along the trail of chocolate he had left. His hands still pressed firmly into my lower back, holding me steady.

My breath came faster but I was still laughing as he

reached my jaw and his licks turned to kisses. His lips reached mine and he stood, pressing himself between my legs, and my mouth opened. My tongue tangled with his, tasting the chocolate he had just removed from my skin. My arms wound around his neck, holding him tightly against me as he deepened the kiss. He finally pulled away, his expression thoughtful.

"What?" I asked.

"The buttercream needed a little more sugar," he said finally, and I scoffed and gave him a shove.

He smirked and reached around me to pluck the two piping bags from the counter. He returned the remaining ganache in the refrigerator and then held up the butter-cream bag. "I can think of another way we can use this."

"You mean because it's not sweet enough for the cupcakes?" I asked.

He cocked a brow before he leaned to pick me up, headed to the stairs. "You ask all the wrong questions."

We fell into my bed. Our lips met again, and we spent the rest of the evening making use of the buttercream.

It tasted sweet enough to me.

THE NEXT DAY found us snuggled in my bed until late morning. Naked from the previous evening's festivities and the knowledge that we were alone for at least another twelve hours when my parents were due to arrive back from my aunt and uncle's place.

I woke to gentle kisses on my bare shoulder and a familiar long-fingered grip on my breast. I stretched, arching my back and pressing myself into the full length of him until he groaned into my neck and rolled to grab a condom from the bedside table. Soon enough he was back behind me, his kisses growing more heated until I turned and caught his mouth with mine. I felt the hardening length of him pressed against my backside and I arched into it again.

He leaned away slightly to slip on the condom before he plunged into me from behind and returned his mouth to mine in a dual melding of tongues and bodies.

I moaned into the kiss and his fingers found their way around my hips and down between my thighs, gently stroking as he thrusted into me. I broke the kiss with a gasp of pleasure, and he smiled against my hair. Slowly I built toward a climax as he took his time, the steady caress of his fingers complimenting the weight of him inside me, until I finally came with a guttural moan and his own orgasm followed shortly until we were both left panting and spent, tangled together in the Sunday sunshine peeking through my curtains.

We lay there for a moment, enjoying the warmth of each other's bodies before I rolled over to face him fully, draping a leg over his hip and pulling him close.

"You know, for a long time I thought I'd imagined how good you were at this," I said, my voice coming out in that slow and languorous tone that follows an amazing orgasm.

"What do you mean?" Benji asked.

"I mean, I thought I was remembering incorrectly. How good our first time was. Everyone says losing your virginity is awkward and uncomfortable, and that just wasn't how it happened for me," I replied.

He leaned away from me, his gaze intent as he studied my face. "Are you telling me that *I* took your virginity?"

I raised an eyebrow at him, a half-smile turned up the corners of my mouth. "Are you telling me you didn't know?"

"Hand on heart, I had no idea." He clutched his chest

and his expression turned very serious. "Shit, you must have thought I was an enormous asshole. Taking your virginity and then hopping off back to Scotland like it was nothing." He paused for a moment and then his eyes widened. "To be clear, it wasn't nothing to me. Ever. I just... I had no idea it was your first time. I would have done some things differently if I'd known."

I squeezed his shoulder reassuringly. "We both handled the aftermath of that badly. It didn't matter that I was a virgin." I shrugged. "Either way, no one else ever quite lived up, and I had convinced myself I had imagined it. I didn't."

I snuggled up next to him and pulled his face down to mine, our lips pressed together, and he seemed to relax into my touch. He pulled back for a moment to whisper, "I'm sorry, Desi."

"I know," I whispered back and pulled him back for more.

14

$\mathscr{I}$ was practically floating that Monday morning as I walked into the office. Things were settling into their rightful place. I felt as though a tremendous weight was lifted off my shoulders.

I thought ending things with Peter would make things easier. That I would be more at ease and feel less guilty for stringing him along this past month. But it hadn't left me feeling better at all.

Now that Benji and I were finally free to be together, now that we had finally confessed those feelings that had been bottled up and ready to explode for the last seven years, I felt optimistic about life for the first time in a very long time. It wasn't as though I had been depressed or living in a bubble since Benji left for Scotland so long ago. I had lived my life. I developed my dreams and passions. I made friends and had lovers. I built my career.

It just hadn't really been... *living.* Today, I felt like a veil was lifted. One that had conspicuously dulled everything in my life. This felt right.

I strolled to my desk with that thought in my head and a

perky jaunt in my step, dropping my bag in the chair before turning in pursuit of my morning coffee.

His back was to me when I entered the break room, and for a moment I considered turning and pretending to use the bathroom so he could finish and leave without this awkward interaction. Before I could do so, his gaze caught me over his shoulder, and he smiled.

"Good morning, Desi," Peter said.

His smile wasn't exactly sad, but it didn't have the bright-eyed joy that it contained in every previous encounter we had like this.

"Good morning, Peter," I replied, shooting a returning smile as I moved to grab a mug from the rack and poured myself a cup. "Just need some fuel, as usual."

"Of course. As usual." He eyed me carefully, and I knew he noticed my particularly positive mood. I was never very good at keeping my thoughts or feelings under wraps. And Peter knew me well. "It seems like you must have had an enjoyable weekend."

I nodded. "Yeah, it was nice."

"Good. Great." His mask began to crack, and the smile faded from his face. He took a swig of his coffee. "Well, have a wonderful week, Desi." And he turned and left the room in haste.

That could have gone worse, I supposed.

I took my coffee back to my desk and worked on checking my emails from the weekend. I spotted one from Jillian titled "Ball-Barlow Project". My heart leapt in my chest and I opened it quickly, scanning the message for the news I had been waiting for and when I found it, the grin stretching across my face could not have been any wider.

"Yes!" I cheered under my breath, pumping my fist toward the ceiling.

Mr. Lincoln Nguyen had chosen Boston House of Design for their upcoming renovation project! This meant a huge bonus for me and the financial freedom I had been planning for over two years. I could finally move out of my parents' house.

My mini-celebration ending, I returned my attention to the email and noted that Mr. Nguyen had decided to come in person for a late morning meeting to finalize the details and Jillian wanted me in attendance. I jotted the time on my calendar and started work preparing the documents we would need for the meeting. The legal staff would work out the contract, obviously, but I decided to put together a portfolio of our plans for Mr. Nguyen to take with him when he left.

The morning flew by as I stayed busy catching up on other projects and before I knew it, Jillian is standing at my desk.

"You ready, Palmer?" she asked, gesturing to the conference room.

"Always," I replied brightly and followed her to the table, the professional portfolio for Lincoln tucked under my arm. She caught sight of it and nodded her approval.

"Good thinking, Desi. Maybe we should have you working on more client liaison business in addition to design. You seem to have a knack for knowing what people will want before anyone needs to ask for it."

My cheeks flushed and I shrugged. "I love design, but I also get a genuine thrill from going above and beyond."

She sat down and I chose the chair across from her as she regarded me with interest. It appeared she may have been about to continue this conversation when the elevator doors opened and Lincoln Nguyen walked out, meeting Tom with a formal but friendly handshake and a warm smile before the two of them made their way to the door of the conference room.

"You remember Jillian, our Vice President of Design. And Desi, our star Junior Design Specialist?" Tom nodded to us, and Lincoln smiled when his gaze caught on mine and suddenly, I couldn't breathe.

"Of course, of course. Nice to see you again, ladies." He broke our eye contact to turn and shake hands with Jillian before settling himself in the chair next to hers while Tom sat next to me.

I almost wished Lincoln had sat next to me rather than directly across the table. I found his presence in my line of vision very distracting. His shoe bumped against my foot under the table, and I hastily tucked my feet back under my chair as Tom and Jillian verbally recounted the terms of the contract that was laid out in front of the young CEO.

He nodded along with their description, flipping through the pages carefully but quickly. He had clearly already seen the document and was only verifying that nothing had been altered. Occasionally his gaze would move from Tom to me, and my cheeks flushed with each glance until he seemed to recognize my discomfort. An eyebrow raised, his generally stoic expression softened into a smile, and he adeptly avoided my eyes for the rest of the contract talk.

Finally, he plucked a pen from his jacket pocket and signed the contract with a flourish, flipping back through to jot his initials where needed on each page before he shuffled the papers together and handed them to Tom. "You'll email over a fully executed copy this afternoon, then?" Lincoln asked and Tom nodded.

"Of course. You'll have it by the end of the day."

Jillian clapped Lincoln on the shoulder. "It's been great

working with you so far, and I'm looking forward to a long and prosperous relationship for both of our companies."

Lincoln reached over to shake her offered hand. "The feeling is mutual, Jillian."

I cleared my throat and turned the portfolio to face Lincoln, sliding it across the table toward him. "Here is a prepared portfolio of everything we went over during the design presentation. It's all still negotiable and open to suggestions, but Jillian and I thought you might want a hard copy to take back with you."

Jillian scoffed. "Oh, please, Desi. Don't sell yourself short."

She turned and placed a hand on Lincoln's shoulder, leaning in as if to whisper a secret. "My colleague here was the one with this brilliant idea; she's just being modest." She grinned at me, and I flushed again before waving her off.

"Anyway, it was nice to see you again, Mr. Nguyen. I'm very excited to be working with you in the future." I stood and offered him my hand, which he took. His head cocked and his expression was unreadable.

"Thank you, Ms. Palmer. We'll be in touch soon, I suppose?" His grip was firm but not overbearing, and his hand was cool and smooth against my clammy palm.

"Of course." I nodded and turned to leave the room, a bit out of sorts after the high I had been riding all morning. I stumbled back to my desk and sank into my chair in relief.

There was something about Lincoln Nguyen that threw me off balance. It was silly. He was just some handsome, rich and powerful CEO. I had read enough romance novels to know not to swoon at those credentials. There was something more to him I could sense just below his measured and careful surface. I couldn't put my finger on it, but he was more than what he seemed, I was sure of it.

Just as I was getting into a good work rhythm I heard a soft knock on my office door. I glanced up and my stomach flipped at the familiar figure standing in the doorway. His face was friendly, and his white teeth gleamed as he smiled warmly at me.

"I hope I'm not bothering you. I was hoping to catch you for a minute before I left." He hesitated, and I snapped back to my default professionalism.

"Have a seat." I gestured at the sole empty chair in the corner of my tiny office and he sat.

He leaned forward in the chair, his elbows on his knees. He was a man with presence, even when seated. He was tall, but it wasn't only his height that added to the weight of him in the enclosed space. His eyes, the color of smoldering coal, were intense as they fixed on me and I did my best not to squirm under his gaze. I had never been alone with him before, I realized.

I cleared my throat. "How can I help you, Mr. Nguyen? Was there a problem with the portfolio?"

"Please, call me Lincoln. And no, the portfolio was perfect. Thank you again." He paused, and I cocked my head.

"Okay, so-" I started.

"I came with a personal request," he started in. "I wondered if you'd be free for dinner Friday night. A chance for Lincoln to get to know Desi. Outside of business."

My chest tightened and those butterflies fluttered again. I swallowed. So Benji had been right after all. I felt so stupid suddenly. How could I be this awful at recognizing romantic interest?

"Oh... um." I cleared my throat again. He must think I was ill as often as I had done so this morning. "I'm flattered, honestly, but I'm seeing someone right now."

He exhaled and leaned back in the chair. "I'm not surprised."

I swallowed again, my cheeks now burning hot at this turn of events, and nodded. "Yes, it's very new. It's actually the chef from the restaurant I took you to for lunch the last time you were in town."

His eyes brightened a bit, and he smiled. "That makes sense. I'm not always the best at reading people, but I thought I sensed something between you two that day."

He stood then, pinning me with another intense look, and seemed to take up even more space in the small room. "Well, anyway. No need to make this anymore awkward. Had to take a shot, right? I promise I won't let this affect our professional relationship."

The breath I had been holding eased in relief at this. "Thanks. I do appreciate that. I am looking forward to that professional relationship." I smiled.

He moved through the doorway and into the hall before pausing for a moment. "And Desi?"

"Yeah?" I asked.

"If anything ever changes, I'll take a rain check on that dinner."

Then he was gone.

I turned back to my desk and dropped my face into my hands, cheeks flushed hot with emotions I couldn't pin down. What in the world was happening to my love life?

15

"*A*h! I am so happy for you, Des!"

I was forced to hold the phone away from my ear due to the sheer volume of Eliza's screeching congratulations. I grinned as I pulled it back to my face. "Thanks, Liza."

"I need all the deets. All of the exciting things happen when I'm out of town." I could almost hear her pout through the phone, and I giggled.

"It's almost like we plan all of our big life events for when you aren't around," I teased, and she scoffed in response.

"I know, it's really rude and inconvenient for me when you do that," she replied but I could hear the smile in her voice now. "So anyway, details?"

I quickly filled her in on what had happened at Carly's 4th of July party. "And then we spent the entire weekend together. It was wonderful. We had the house to ourselves since my parents were in Maine."

"Spent the weekend together doing what exactly?" Eliza asked.

"Liza, I'm not giving you a play by play," I said firmly.

"Fine, fine. I just had an amazing weekend of hotel sex, so I guess I don't *need* it to tide me over or anything," she replied.

"I still need to talk to my parents about it. I mean, right? I should tell them? What's the protocol on starting to officially date your childhood friend who is like a son to your parents while still living in their house?" I mused.

"You've got to get out of your parents' house, Desi," Eliza said. "You've just got that big bonus, right? I can help you find a place! Oh! I think there might be an apartment available in my building. That would be awesome to be so close again. Just hop down the elevator to see you? It'd be just like when we were kids."

"Oh, that *would* be amazing! Your building is awesome and so close to work. Send me the details, and I'll try to get started on that," I replied. "But you didn't help me with my parent problem."

"Eh, I think they'll be fine. You're going to have to tell them though; they aren't blind. They'll notice something's up and that would be even more awkward."

I sighed. "You're right. So not looking forward to this."

"Does Kira know?" Eliza asked, and my stomach lurched at the sound of Kira's name. I had been purposely ignoring the Kira factor in this situation.

"Er. I don't know actually," I said.

Eliza tutted. "Desi, you can't keep avoiding awkward conversations. I know you and Kira haven't been seeing eye to eye lately, but she's one of your oldest friends. Don't you think she deserves to hear it from you?"

"You're right, as always. I'll try to figure out how to talk to her about it." I rubbed my face, imagining just how painful that conversation was going to be. "Anyway, we are on for poker night at your place this week, right?"

"Right. I'll see you and your lover then."

I cackled. "See you then!"

There was a reason I called Eliza first. She always told me what I needed to hear and not just what I wanted to hear.

I turned to make my way to the kitchen to find my parents, my mind spinning with how to bring this up without it being the most awkward conversation of my life. However, my gaze fell immediately on my mother, grinning.

"Oh, hi, Mom," I said, and she held her arms wide.

"I'm just so happy for you, baby!" she gushed, pulling me into a hug. "Your father is going to be thrilled."

"Er... what?" I asked.

"You and Benji!" she said in my ear, and I scoffed.

"Ma! Eavesdropping, really?" I exclaimed and she chuckled as she pulled away from me.

"Desi, your voice carries and you were standing in the middle of the living room having your little phone call." She winked and started back to the kitchen with me following along behind her, face blazing in embarrassment.

"How much did you hear, exactly?"

"Enough. Don't worry about it. Just come, sit, dinner is ready."

I slid into a chair at the table and started filling my plate as my mom settled herself across the table from me. She hollered across the house for my dad to join us. Once he was settled beside my mother, she elbowed him, a conspiratorial smile on her lips.

"Desi has some news for us."

I groaned. "Mom. Please."

"You're finally moving out?" Dad guessed and I covered my face with my hands.

"Ugh. Not the time, Dad. But yes, I'm going to start looking for a place."

"No, not that, Clay." She swatted at him and he laughed. She turned her earnest gaze back to me. "And, baby, you know you can stay here as long as you need."

"I know, Mom. Thanks."

"Desi and Benji are finally together," my mother said, beaming, her hands clasped to her chest. My dad's smile faded.

"Seriously?" he asked.

"Seriously," Mom replied.

He turned his attention back to me, his expression shocked and unsmiling, and my stomach flipped. *Here it comes.* I thought I had known what kind of reaction to expect from him, but the look on his face didn't seem to be positive. Not like my mother, still grinning widely at me. His eyes shimmered.

"Dad, are you crying?" I asked and he swiped at his eyes and stood, closing the distance around the table to pull me up into a tight hug.

"I'm so happy for you, baby! This is great news." His arms were so tightly wrapped around me that it was getting hard to breathe.

"Dad... Dad, loosen up a bit." He stepped back, his hands resting on my shoulders.

"I was beginning to think you two wouldn't ever figure it out."

LATER THAT EVENING, when Benji made it back to the house after closing down the restaurant, we were lying in my bed catching up on the day. Every so often he would reach over and run his fingers across my arm, or my shoulder. A casual intimacy that left goosebumps across my skin and sent the butterflies going in my stomach.

My bedroom door was open, and my parents were just down the stairs watching a movie in the living room. I felt like a teenager again. *I really need to get out of this house.*

"So... your parents know now?" he asked after a few moments of silence had fallen.

I nodded. "Yep."

"I thought they were looking at me a little funny when I came through the door."

"Dad's exact words were 'I was beginning to think you two wouldn't ever figure it out'." I curled my fingers in air quotes around the statement, and Benji chuckled.

"He should leave me out of that one. I've had it figured out for a while." He grabbed my hand and laced our fingers together, leaning in to place a gentle kiss on my lips. He was warm and smelled like freshly baked bread, and I melted into him as he deepened the kiss, his arm sliding around to my back to press me firmly against him.

My free hand found a grip on the back of his neck and I felt goosebumps prickle his skin at the caress. My stomach flipped again, my breaths coming faster. Knowing he reacted to my touch in the same way I reacted to his was intoxicating.

He finally pulled away, his smile wide and his eyes gleaming. He rubbed his nose against mine. "What? No clap-back for that one, lass?"

My brain was still swimming. "Hm?"

"That I had it figured out for a while?"

I scoffed. "Yeah, yeah. Desi's the dense one. Got it."

He snuggled his face into my neck, laughing and leaving another trail of prickling goosebumps on my skin as his hot breath breezed past. Almost involuntarily I pulled him against me, wanting more than anything to just be wrapped up in him.

"Just another thing I like about you," he whispered into my ear, and I turned to press another deep kiss to his mouth. I rolled on top of him, my knees pinned his hips to the bed and his hands drew slow, shiver-inducing strokes across my lower back, exposed from my sudden movement. I moaned into his mouth and he ran his hands up my back and tangled his fingers into my hair.

Without a thought I ground myself down against him and felt his body responding under me. I smiled against his mouth and, coming to my senses, pulled away. His hands were still wrapped in my hair and he tried to pull me back to him.

"Benji," I whispered, my voice thick with desire, "my parents are like thirty feet away downstairs."

He groaned and leaned up on his elbows, hands falling from my hair to the bed. He placed a last kiss to my bare shoulder. "You're right. We should at least wait until they are asleep."

The past weekend had been bliss. It was going to be more difficult to have so much uninterrupted time moving forward with the current living situation.

"It's a date. Same place, twelve o'clock?" I asked.

"I'll be here."

I STARED at the phone in my hands. The contact was pulled up and taunting me every time I glanced down. Kira.

I took a deep breath. I'd been putting this off for too long now, and I needed to get it behind me. I knew there was a possibility that our nearly lifelong friendship, already on the rocks, would be over after this conversation. My stomach was in knots.

Finally, I pressed the button to make the call and brought the phone to my ear, the ringing mocking me as my heart beat even faster.

Then a click and Kira's clipped voice cut through the incessant ringing.

"Hello, Desi. I was wondering when you were going to call," she answered.

"Hey, Kira," I started but then my voice seemed to catch in my throat.

"I'd have thought you'd have a long speech prepared filled with your excuses. I guess maybe you aren't as predictable as I thought."

The venom in her voice was enough to make my stomach heave. I really didn't want to have this conversation.

"I'm sorry. I know the way this shook out was really shitty." I managed to find my voice again, and she laughed coldly.

"Yeah, you're always sorry. That never stops you from taking whatever you want," she replied, and I swallowed hard to quell the anger that bubbled up at that ridiculous accusation.

"I know you're hurt. I'm sorry that what I did hurt you. I'm sorry that my timing was so awful for everyone involved." My courage returned, and my voice was firm and pointed now. "I am sorry that you got caught in the crossfire,

Kira. You knew better than anyone how strongly I felt about him."

"Yes. Yes, I did. Seven fucking years ago, Desi. You had a boyfriend. You never said a fucking thing about still carrying a torch for Benji. I'll be honest, I was blindsided by this. You aren't getting a pass just because you're taking the high road and apologizing. For what? Stealing my guy? Fucking him not even twenty-four hours after he had ended things with me?" Her anger was growing, and her words were coming faster, more frantic. "No, fuck that, Desi. I'm not even close to forgiving you."

"That's fair," I replied simply over the lump growing once more in my throat. I deserved this. I wasn't going to argue with her.

"And to think, all of this for a guy who is temporary. He's going back to London in what? Six weeks? Eight? He and I had an understanding about this being a summer thing. We knew and agreed it was temporary for while he was here." She spat the words. "I don't think that's at all what you're looking for from him... good luck with that."

I didn't even know what to say to that. On one hand, it didn't make much sense for her to be this angry with me if that was true and they had both agreed to a temporary relationship. On the other hand, she was right. That was not the relationship I was looking for.

I'd been so caught up in trying to figure out how I felt about him after all of this time. And after finally sorting that out, if I should even tell him. And then how to tell him. I hadn't dwelled long on the very temporary nature of his presence in Boston.

I could ask him to stay. Could I ask him to stay? Was that even a fair request to make after such a short time together? My mind was now reeling with doubts and my stomach was so twisted up that I thought I might vomit.

"Goodbye, Desi," Kira said with finality, and the click that followed told me she had hung up.

16

*P*oker night turned into more of a triple date night that week. Kira was, understandably, absent. Meredith, one quarter of our usual serious poker players, was still caught up at work and couldn't make it. This left me, Harvey, and Liam trying to play a serious game around Carly and Eliza, who never took it seriously, and Benji, who had a singular goal of teasing me whenever possible.

In the end, we played only a few hands and shifted into drinking games much earlier than usual.

At some point during the night, the men all converged on the patio for some fresh air and "man-talk", as Liam jokingly referred to it, which left me in a rosy buzzed state snuggled between my two good friends on Eliza's worn sofa.

"I'm so happy for you, babe," Carly said once the guys were out of earshot, squeezing my knee and grinning at me. "You guys are so adorable."

"Oh my god, right? Thank fuck they finally admitted what we have all seen for fucking months," Eliza exclaimed.

"You're clearly already drunk, Liza," I giggled. Her potty mouth was never completely under wraps, but it always ramped up when she had a little too much to drink.

"Is this a surprise to you when I'm hosting poker night?" She smirked.

"Don't tell Liam I told you this but... he totally said he didn't think Peter was your type the first time we met him. I mean, he was nice, but he was a little too... corporate. Or something. Can't quite put my finger on it, but he wasn't right for you," Carly mused.

"I think it's just because we could all sense the palpable sexual chemistry brewing between Desi and that Scottish joker outside," Eliza chimed in, jerking her thumb in the direction of the patio. "Don't know why Kira even bothered; it was so obvious."

"Kira said she had no idea I still had feelings for him," I said.

"Oh, you talked to her then?" Eliza asked. "How'd that go?"

"About as well as you'd expect. She's pissed. I don't know if she'll forgive me for it." I shrugged, but tears stung my eyes. I blinked them away. "She said they had some agreement that this was just a summer thing, so I don't know why she's this upset."

Eliza's eyebrows flew up at this. Her eyes widened. "Oh, really? Interesting. Because he was going to be going back to London, you mean?"

The reminder of Benji's imminent departure made my stomach flip, and I simply nodded.

Eliza frowned. Her brow furrowed in thought.

"What?" I asked.

"Oh nothing, it's nothing. I'm sure it will turn out fine.

Kira will cool down eventually," Eliza said, wrapping an arm around my shoulder and pulling me into a side hug.

"She will. I know it," Carly encouraged. "Besides, she knew Benji was still hung up on you. She told me so herself."

"Wait, what? She knew?" I asked, surprised. "For how long?"

"Oh, since the very beginning, basically," Carly replied.

"Why didn't you say anything?" I sat up and turned toward her.

"Well, I did. I just didn't say that Kira told me," she said.

"When?" I asked.

"The night we all met Peter, remember. I told you Benji was crazy about you."

"What? But I thought you were just saying that based on observation like everyone else." My brain whirled with this extra information.

"Kira made me swear not to tell anyone, so I couldn't just tell you how I knew," Carly countered. "I do have *some* chill, Desi."

"So, she knew, before they even started anything, that he still had feelings for me?" I thought back to that evening. How Kira had cozied up to Benji. How she'd pulled him off and got him alone. Then I remembered the question she had asked during Never Have I Ever. *Have you ever slept with a coworker?*

And Peter and I had both taken a drink. Shit. Benji must have decided then that things were serious between me and Peter and that he didn't have a chance. Even though the coworkers in question were not each other.

"She has no right to be angry with me," I fumed. "She manipulated this whole thing from the beginning."

"Yeah, that's all pretty fucking shady if you ask me," Eliza agreed.

My anger surged even through my semi-drunken haze. Slowly, I took a breath and exhaled.

"At this point, it doesn't matter. At least I can stop feeling so guilty about how things happened, I guess. What's done is done," I said, and my friends sandwiched me in a hug.

The men returned in a chorus of laughter and the mood in the room brightened once more. Benji settled in a chair across the room, and I drifted over to sit on his lap. Once settled I wrapped my arms around his neck and kissed him deeply, not caring that we weren't alone in the room. He squeezed my waist and when I broke away from his lips, he caught my gaze, his eyes questioning.

"Everything okay, lass?" he asked.

I nodded. "Everything is perfect."

TIME SEEMED endless for the next few weeks. I effectively pushed worries about Benji returning to London out of my mind... mostly.

We had known each other well growing up and, despite the years apart, had already fallen back into our usual repertoire even before we had decided to be together as an official couple. That left more time for forging a physical relationship, and we didn't shy away from doing just that. It was exciting and felt forbidden since we were both still living under my parents' roof.

Not that either of my parents were stupid enough to not know what was going on. The sneaking around still added an air of intrigue. Making out in my bed, careful not to make too much noise to alert the others in the house. Waiting until midnight for Benji to sneak into my room. We were having a blast.

One evening, after a particularly heavy make-out session, we decided we were famished and made our way down to the kitchen for some re-fueling. We devoured some leftover pasta from the refrigerator and the rest of a pan of brownies Benji had made earlier in the week.

After cleaning up after ourselves, we were pulled back to one another like magnets. My arms snaked around his neck and a smirk played on my face as he raised an eyebrow at me mischievously.

"What's going on in that head of yours?" I asked, instantly suspicious.

He didn't bother to reply and with his hands on my hips he walked me backward until the countertop bumped against my rear-end.

"Not fair." I pouted at him as I looked up at his now grin-ning face from under my lashes.

"Who said I was playing fair?" he teased as his fingers found the bottom of my cotton nightshirt and started working it upwards, warm fingers brushing the outside of my thighs as he did.

My cheeks flushed. "We shouldn't, my parents are upstairs."

"They are definitely asleep, lass. It's late." He dipped his head to kiss my neck, and I inhaled sharply, pressing my hips into him as I tilted my head back.

He smiled against my neck as he continued riding the hem of my nightie higher until his voyaging fingers could move freely between my thighs. I pressed my fist to my mouth as I let out a moan. He brought one hand up to grasp my wrist and pulled my fist away, his lips on my mouth muffling my moans as his fingers slipped under my underwear.

His tongue flicked expertly over my own, his breathing growing more labored.

He pulled away for a moment, his hands gripped my hips, turning me so I was facing away from him. I leaned heavily into the countertop as he hiked my shirt the rest of the way over my hips, his fingers reached around to find my sweet spot again as his lips returned to my neck and he pressed himself against my ass. His arousal was obvious through the cotton of his sweatpants. I moaned again.

"I want you to fuck me," I said, managing the words without my voice shaking, though his urgent fingers between my legs and his fervent kisses on my neck threatened to break the last shred of control I had left. I pressed my lips together and arched into him again.

"But your parents are just upstairs..." he teased as he slipped a finger into me, his other hand wrapping around my jaw, offering his fingers for me to use. I opened my mouth and closed my lips around them to muffle my gasp.

I pressed my ass more firmly into his growing arousal, and he groaned.

"Stop being a tease," I said, my voice thick with desire but almost a whisper.

"As you wish." He pulled a condom from his pocket and lowered his pants to slip it on. I leaned forward further on the counter as he pushed aside my underwear and plunged into me with a small, satisfied sigh.

His arm wrapped around my waist, holding me securely as he leaned his weight forward, his breath hot on my neck as he growled into my hair. "You are the perfect woman, Desi." I tilted my hips in response to give him a better angle, my own moans muffled against my arm.

"Please, don't stop. Oh god."

"Not planning to, lass," he whispered, and my climax built and built with each thrust. His teeth grazed my bare shoulder, and this sent me over the edge. His hand found my mouth again, offering himself as the sacrifice to my teeth to ensure the entire house didn't hear just how incredible he was making me feel.

I clamped down on his hand once more to keep from crying out and he hissed and groaned behind me, his own orgasm coming on top of my own.

We are both still for a moment, panting and spent, before he leaned back and put my clothing to rights. I still could not quite trust my legs, my weight held against the counter. He fixed himself up before stooping to scoop me up, my eyes heavy as I leaned my head into his shoulder.

My arms found their place around his neck as I nuzzled my face under his chin, feeling tears prick my eyes for reasons I couldn't explain. "I fucking love you," I whispered, planting an open mouth kiss at his throat. He swallowed heavily as he carried me to the bedroom.

"I fucking love you too, lass."

17

I drank my coffee in the living room that weekend, a fresh romance novel in my lap. Saturday, my favorite day of the week. No commitments and knowing that when I fell asleep later that night, I still wouldn't have to go back to reality yet the next day.

Benji slipped into the room with his own steaming mug of tea, and he settled beside me on the sofa as I read, sipping in silence, his free hand reached over to rest on my bare thigh. We sat like that for a moment, and I felt a twinge of longing at this tiny glimpse of what life could be.

"My boss is in town today, lass."

That snapped me out of it. I dog-eared the page to mark my place and set the book and my coffee mug on the end table.

"Yeah? You just found out about this?" That was a little alarming. "Is something wrong at the restaurant?"

His expression is sheepish, and he removed his hand from my leg to run it across his head. "Well, no. I've known he was coming for a few weeks now."

I raised my eyebrow, studying him intently and trying to find the words to respond to this revelation.

"I see."

Why hadn't he told me until just now? I had a sinking feeling in my stomach at this news, though I couldn't quite put my finger on why it bothered me.

"Want to tag along with me, then? Meet the mysterious man who has given me such power and responsibility?" He grinned. "He has already asked to meet you."

I tapped my finger against my chin, pretending to think about this. "I just don't know. Maybe if I had known a few weeks ago, I would have been better able to arrange my schedule for this."

In a quick movement, Benji sat his own mug safely on the coffee table and had wrapped me in his arms, pinning me to the sofa. I couldn't keep the laugh from my throat as he covered my neck with kisses and nuzzled my shoulder. "Please, lass. I need you to come."

I let out a final giggle before I fake-sighed. "I suppose I can make room in my very busy day for you." I pressed a finger to his nose as he grinned down at me. I was smiling, but my brain was already whirring away with what exactly this visit meant.

An hour later and we were in my car heading to the restaurant. Even though Benji was driving, I had a sudden flashback to that moment earlier in the summer right after he'd arrived. Him asleep in the passenger seat. Me alone with my thoughts and trying to sort through all the feelings swirling around in my head.

I had finally gotten them sorted out, but the unshake-able feeling of foreboding twisting in my belly made me think they were about to be turned on their head again.

We found parking just down the street from the restaurant and we emerged from the car and headed down the sidewalk. Benji sidled up to me, grabbing my hand and twining his fingers through mine. I smiled, despite that sense of dread still lingering in my stomach, and turned to plant a kiss on his cheek. I thought I could see him flush red for a moment under those freckles I loved so much. On the face I loved so much. On the man I loved so much.

My stomach flipped again as I tried not to think about what this meeting with Benji's boss might mean for us. I squeezed his hand and he squeezed back, reassuringly.

"Are you alright, Desi?" he asked, and I nodded, forcing myself to smile.

"Of course. Let's go meet the man behind the legend," I said.

We made our way into the restaurant, and Benji nodded to the hostess before leading me to the private room in the back that was typically reserved for business lunches or family parties. We entered the room, and a man was already seated in the back, a cell phone to his ear and his free hand rubbing his temples as he spoke.

He was well muscled and tanned, and his accent was obviously British. I wasn't well versed in the nuances of the variations of a British accent, but his was less royal family and more Mary Poppins chimney sweep. "... alright, well I'm in Boston through Monday and I should be able to meet with him Tuesday, then. You'll set it up? Wonderful. You're a doll. Thanks, Grace."

He hung up and turned his face up to us. He was both younger and older than I had expected. His crystal blue eyes were bright, his hair and beard were dark but riddled with gray specks. He grinned widely and stood when he spotted Benji.

"Benny boy!" he exclaimed and wrapped Benji in a tight

bear hug. Benji grinned against the taller, bulkier man's shoulder.

"Welcome to Boston, Hank." He leaned away from the man and slapped his shoulder companionably before stepping back to reach his arm back for me. I took his hand and nodded at the large man. "This is Desi."

The man's gaze took me in, warm and friendly, and he nodded his approval. "Well done, lad. She's beautiful." He reached a large pink hand out toward me, and I released Benji's long fingers and returned the handshake firmly. This made his eyes widen a bit in surprise. "A proper handshake, too. I'm impressed. How'd you manage to land this one, Benji?"

Benji's grin was wider than I'd ever seen it. "Lucked out, I guess." He winked at me and the three of us settled into our seats at the table and a waitress appeared to take our orders for lunch.

Benji and Hank got right into discussing business and how the restaurant was coming along. I sipped my lemonade, only partly following the discussion while I tried to will the pit in my stomach to go away. Finally, I caught the words I'd been dreading all day.

"... it sounds like you've gotten everything running smoothly. If you're as confident in the staff as you say, I really need you back in London. Do you think you could make the arrangements to fly back late next week, then? We've got a huge conference we are catering next weekend, and I could use you to help coordinate day-of."

I froze and closed my eyes at these words. Pressing my lips together and willing my eyes not to fill with tears when I opened them again.

"Desi, lass? Are you okay?" I heard Benji's concerned voice as though I was underwater. It was far away, fading, disappearing. Just like Benji himself. I swallowed and forced my eyes open, nodding.

"Yeah. I'm alright." I pushed my chair back from the table. "I think I just need a moment. I'll be in the ladies room." I stood and fled to the bathroom, barely holding it together before the door closed behind me and I could fall apart in peace. He was leaving. Of course he was leaving. He was always going to leave.

He was always going to leave me.

I leaned my head back against the bathroom door, tears streaming down my face as I tried to loosen the knot in my chest, at least enough that I could go back to the table and get through this lunch without looking like a complete mess. I heard a soft tapping from the other side of the door.

"Desi? Are you sure you're alright?" Benji asked softly.

I composed myself more before answering. "Yes, Benji. I'll be out in a minute."

"Let me in, lass."

I swiped at my face, knowing it would not do much good when my eyes were already red and puffy from the tears. I opened the door a crack, and he slipped through, wrapping his arms around me tightly and pulling me to his chest as it clicked closed again. I hadn't been expecting this, and the gesture brought a fresh round of tears to my eyes.

"Shh. Babe, it's going to be alright." He stroked my hair and pressed a kiss to my forehead.

"No. It's not. You're leaving." I got the words out without crumpling into sobs, but the knot in my chest tightened up again at the words finally being said out loud.

"We've got a whole week. Can't we just enjoy it?"

I leaned away from him, my brow knitting in anger as I brought my eyes to his face.

"Are you serious right now? That's how you comfort me

when I'm upset that I'm losing you, *again*? What the *fuck*, Benji?"

This rendered him speechless, and his defeated expression softened my anger a bit. I turned to the sink and ran the cold water, wetting my hands and then scrubbing them across my face. I breathed deeply for a few moments until I finally felt more in control of my emotions.

"Let's just get through this lunch and we can talk about it later. Your boss is probably already wondering what we are up to together in the bathroom for this long," I said, my voice steady again.

He nodded, his face giving nothing away. "Alright, then." He opened the door and gestured for me to go first, and we headed back to our table.

We made it through the rest of lunch with no further incident. The conversation had turned from business to personal, and I even found myself laughing at the easy back and forth the two men shared. It was clear they knew each other well and shared a mutual respect. I realized that I knew very little about what Benji's life was like back in London. Or what his life had been like since I had last seen him.

I knew the highlights, of course, but how did he spend his days? Who did he spend them with? He was in London, his parents in Edinburgh, his sister in Glasgow. I had barely heard mention of anything other than his job in the entire summer he'd been here.

My cheeks flushed a bit at this realization, and I was ashamed of myself for not taking a more active interest in his life. I had been so focused on my own job and all of these complicated feelings resurfacing that I had not bothered to ask. It was no wonder he was just accepting that we'd be done next week after enjoying this last blissful month together.

We finished up lunch, and Benji and Hank shook hands. "I'll give you the details on my travel plans once I have them, Hank. I'll see you next week." We said our good-byes and headed back to the car. The easy and intimate way we had entered the restaurant had been shattered by the countdown to our separation. My arms were wrapped around myself protectively and we walked in silence.

We both got into the car and got a few minutes into the drive back before he started to speak.

"I think we need to get a few things straight here, lass."

"Yes, I think we do," I agreed. "I thought when we found out you were going back to London, we'd have weeks to figure out where to go from there. It's days. Days, Benji. I can't-"

"Do you want out of this already? Is that it?" he asked, anger creeping into his voice though he keeps his tone level.

I recoiled at this accusation.

"This is exactly what happened before, Desi." He took a deep breath.

"What are you talking about? That was entirely different," I shot back.

"Was it?" he asked. Turning his gaze toward me for a moment, his own eyes glistening with tears he refused to let spill down his face. He quickly looked away again, returning his attention to the road.

I thought about it for a moment. We had hooked up and afterwards something had shifted. Something felt different. Maybe it *had* been me. Maybe I had pushed him away, knowing he was leaving soon. Wanting to protect myself from hurting with his absence. I had convinced myself at the time that Benji had regretted our night together. We hadn't talked about it all, anyway. And he had gone back home to Scotland a few weeks later.

I had assumed he had gotten what he wanted and was satisfied with that. We were just friends, after all. And turning it into more was complicated, especially with the distance.

But maybe I had been wrong. I knew when we had last spoken about our first time it had surprised him to know I had been a virgin. He had said he would have done some things differently if he had known. What exactly had that meant? I hadn't dwelled on it much at the time, but now it seemed significant.

We pulled into the driveway and headed inside, Benji still clearly upset as he took our leftover food to the kitchen while I stood, lost in thought, in the living room. My arms still crossed across my chest. Trying to steady my breathing.

"I thought... I thought it hadn't mattered to you," I whispered when he stepped into the living room and he froze at my words, his hands clenched into fists at his sides and his eyes blazing with a heat I'd never seen before.

"Damn it, Desi. What kind of lad do you take me for? You thought it didn't matter? You thought it meant nothing to me? I already told you it was *never* nothing for me." His face wavered between anger and hurt, and I felt my stomach lurch at the sight.

"We... we never talked about it. After. I thought that's what you wanted. To pretend it never happened." My nails dug into my upper arms as I fought to hold back my tears.

"None of this has gone the way I wanted." He exhaled. "And it's just as much my fault as it is yours. I have never been great at talking about how I really feel. I make jokes, I brush it under the rug. I don't talk about it, though. Defense mechanism, I guess."

He shook his head, his expression softening into something more thoughtful and less on the edge of white-hot rage. The silence lingered for a moment before he spoke again, slowly and clearly. Each word chosen carefully, and the intensity of his feelings packed into each syllable.

"I mean it's bloody stupid. It's daft. It's insanity, really. That you can think about someone so much and so often when you haven't seen their face in seven years. Right? It's crazy to think about someone *that* much. To wonder how they are, what they are doing... hell, *who* they are. Seven years is a long time to still be thinking about someone. Dreaming about them. Wanting them. That's me. I'm insane."

I paused a beat, letting him stew in the silence for a minute as he searched my face for my reaction to this speech.

"Wow..." I exhaled as I let the word slip out. His gaze was earnest, a flicker of hope behind the mask of irritation. "I didn't know Kira had made such an impression on you the last time you were here."

"Oh, bloody hell, Desi. You're impossible." He shook his head, lowering himself to the couch where he stared at his hands. His forehead creased in frustration. The light-hearted teasing hadn't broken the tension as I had hoped it would.

"The whole time? You wanted me the whole time?" I whispered the question. My chest is tight with this new knowledge that it hadn't just been me pining away all these years.

He turned his gaze up to mine. "Yes, the whole fucking time."

His eyes gleamed with a mixture of annoyance and desire as I moved closer to him, taking his face in my hands to turn his eyes up toward me where I stood in front of him.

"Me too," I breathed.

With those words he pulled me swiftly down to his lap, his hands in my hair and his mouth on mine. I wrapped myself around him like it was the most natural place in the world for me to be, rocking myself against him. His breath was hot on my neck as he broke our kiss for his lips to explore the rest of me. I threw my head back and moaned at the sensation as he pulled my sleeve down over my shoulder until my left breast was free and his mouth found the now bare flesh. My hands held his head to me as he maneuvered me off his lap and onto my back on the sofa, pulling the hem of my skirt up past my hips as his mouth continued to work at my breast.

I moaned again as his fingers flickered between my legs, over my panties, and I felt him smile against my chest. He released me and looked up at my face, his eyes slanted with his grin and his cheeks flushed. "Be still now, lass," he directed as he moved down my body, his breath now hot against the inside of my thigh. I shivered involuntarily as he planted a kiss right on my sweet spot. "I said be still." He winked at me from between my legs as I tried to regain some of my composure.

A silly thing to attempt as he deftly moved a finger under my panties and inside of me, already slick with wetness. His grin spread wide again at this realization.

"The whole time," he whispered into my thigh. The tickle of his breath made me twitch as I tried to keep still, and the words sent a surge of pleasure and heat down my spine. He sat up to remove my underwear completely and then returned to replace his fingers with his tongue. I cried out, my body aching to writhe beneath him, but his hands were now firmly holding my thighs in place as his mouth moved so frustratingly slowly. I whined and moaned as the desire built in my belly.

"Benji..." I managed the word, and he looked up at me again, his eyes shining with need.

"Yes?" He murmured the question between my legs only making me need him more.

"Please, I want you..."

He cocked a brow at this and licked me one last time before he stood to undo his own pants, sliding the condom on as he pulled me up and on top of him.

I slid onto him in one swift motion and cried out with relief at him filling me. He sighed at the coupling, returning his attention to my free breast as I moved up and down at a breakneck pace, needing to finish what he'd started as he panted underneath me, losing himself.

He moaned into my shoulder, abandoning any need to continue to pleasure me while I rode him hard to finish us both. He scraped his teeth across my bare shoulder, claiming me as I drew my fingers hard across his back. Gasping we came together, and breathing heavily, we collapsed beside each other on the sofa.

"Fuck, Benji," I breathed as he placed tender kisses on my neck.

"Yes, you did." He grinned. "Very well."

18

Two days to go. Just two more days with him and I was feeling the pressure. The fact that nothing seemed to affect Benji only made things worse for me. It's like we hadn't received the news that this little affair was about to come to an abrupt end. He hadn't even brought up the fact he was leaving since the day we had received the news from Hank. It made me feel insane.

I was having difficulty concentrating at work. Every hour that ticked by brought me that much closer to Benji's departure, and I couldn't even spend it with him because I was stuck in the office. He had quickly wrapped up his lingering responsibilities at the restaurant and was spending most of his remaining time trekking around Boston and doing the vacation activities he'd been unable to do in the whirlwind of managing a successful restaurant opening.

I received a message from him that afternoon at work, "Frank's at 7?", and even though it had brightened my day momentarily, the weight wasn't lifted for long. We needed to have a serious discussion very soon. I hated this feeling of being in limbo, of not knowing what next week, much less the entire future, was going to bring.

I pulled into the parking lot and spotted him leaning casually against the side of the building, hands in his pockets. I smiled, the sight of him enough to lift my spirits even with the gnawing pit in my stomach of the looming conversation. I parked the car and made my way to the door.

"Come here often?" I asked, and he grinned at me. My heart flipped. Was it ever going to stop doing that?

"Only to see the pretty girls," he said, and he reached for my hand. "Can I interest you in a Belgian waffle?"

I laughed, and we strolled inside together. We settled into our usual booth and ordered within minutes. Our usual meal. Benji regaled me with the news of his day. As he spoke, my optimism slowly dissipated as that pit in my stomach grew larger and darker.

"Is everything alright, lass? I feel like I've lost you."

I realized I'd picked up the paper napkin from the table and have twisted it into a mangled mess. I felt his hand on my arm and looked up at him. He smiled, but there was concern shining in his eyes.

"What are we doing here, Benji?" I finally asked.

"What do you mean?" he replied, his forehead wrinkling. "I thought we were having dinner." His joke didn't have quite the same usual light-hearted tone. I flashed him an annoyed glare.

"I just mean... you're going back to London. My life is here. Is that even something that can work?" He visibly stiffened at these words, but I forced myself to continue. "Are we wasting our time?"

His hand on the table clenched into a fist as his jaw tightened, "Can't we just enjoy these next few days, Desi?"

I swallowed hard. Knowing that a few more days weren't

ever going to be enough for me. Knowing if I didn't try to get some closure in this last bit of time with him that I might never recover from the heartbreak that followed. I didn't understand how he could be so cavalier about this, knowing the time we had left was so short.

"Benji. I just don't want either of us getting hurt by how this ends." My eyes prickled, and I fought back the tears, not wanting to make a scene in front of everyone in the diner. Benji raised his hand to the waitress.

"Can we get our food boxed up and the check, please?"

"Benji don't be like this," I retorted, my face now flushed with irritation.

"Desi. We need to have this out, and I'm not doing it here."

The waitress bagged up our meals. Benji paid the check, and we both headed out to my car. His posture was still stiff with irritation, something I had only seen once before after our meeting with Hank.

We settled into our seats, and I started the short drive home, the tense silence only deepened that dark pit in my stomach. I pulled up in front of the house and parked the car but I didn't turn it off. My parents were home, and this wasn't a conversation that needed an audience.

"I can't do this, Benji." My words sliced through the tension and my heart squeezed in response to them. I couldn't look at him. My gaze remained on my hands still resting on the steering wheel.

He exhaled and I could see him in my peripheral vision shaking his head, his hands raised to rub his face in frustration.

"I don't know why I thought this time would be any different," he said, finally. His voice coming out in a strangled sound I had never heard before. My heart squeezed some more, and my throat was tight. "Can you at least look at me, Desi?"

With some effort I turned my head, my gaze cast down at his bouncing knee for a moment before I found the courage to meet his eyes. It almost broke me, the look on his face. Hurt, loss, betrayal. I did that to him. But this was better for both of us. Closure was better than the unending years of "what if" that would follow if we didn't end this with a clean break now. I couldn't go through that again.

"I'm sorry. I'm so sorry," I whispered through the tightness in my throat. My eyes filled with tears.

"Then take it back. Please take it back." He reached for my hands, and I let him take them. I squeezed his fingers gently before placing them back in his lap as I leaned away.

"You don't know how badly I want to do that, Ben. But I can't. This is how this was always going to end, right? You were always going back. I was always staying here."

A few tears slipped down my cheek, and I saw in his face he was fighting not to reach out and brush them away. I lifted my hand and wiped at them myself. He turned away from me then, and without another word he got out of the car and walked inside. I collapsed into sobs as soon as he was through the door and cried alone in my car for everything we might have been if things were different. I allowed myself ten minutes to fall apart completely and then I wiped off my face, grabbed the bag with our takeout, and headed inside myself.

It was still early, but I was so emotionally spent that I popped our food into the refrigerator and then told my wide-eyed parents that I was going to bed early before I escaped to my bedroom. I pulled the curtains closed and changed into sweatpants and an old ratty tee before climbing under the covers. I had held it together for the song and dance for my parents, but in the safety and privacy of my bedroom, I crumbled into sobs once more and eventually fell asleep.

During the night I woke to the creak of my door opening and Benji's warm, familiar presence appeared next to me beneath the blankets. Instinctively, as I had many nights in the past few weeks, I turned and reached for him, and he wrapped his arms around me, breathing into my hair before pressing a kiss to my forehead. I snuggled into his embrace, and we both fell asleep once more.

BENJI WAS GONE before I woke up the next morning.

I had gotten up early and took a long bath to relax before getting myself put together for work. Finally, I had wandered down the hallway to Cy's bedroom where Benji had stayed most of the summer. On the nights we hadn't spent together, anyway.

I raised my hand and knocked before I pushed open the door. It took me a few moments to realize what I saw. The room was empty of Benji's things. It took another moment to realize what that meant, and I sank to the mattress in disbelief. I heard footsteps in the hall, but I couldn't seem to process anything outside of this hollow feeling that had taken up residence in my chest.

"You alright, love?"

My dad's voice sounded very far away, but I looked up at him leaning against the door frame and I nodded, swallowing hard and clasping my hands together in my lap.

"Change of plans then?" I asked.

"He said this morning that his boss wanted him back as

soon as possible. He was done with the restaurant anyway and had checked off all of his Boston tourist destinations, so he got his flight moved up," he replied. His voice was steady and matter-of-fact, but his brow was wrinkled with concern. He didn't quite believe me when I said I was alright.

"Right, I guess that makes sense." I couldn't bring myself to stand and leave the room yet. There was still a ghost of him in this space.

My dad took this cue to lower himself next to me and he wrapped an arm around me, pulling me close as I leaned my head against his sturdy shoulder. He kissed the top of my head and whispered, "I know you love him, Desi. I'm not sure what happened, but I know this can't be easy for you. I'm here if you need to talk about it."

I nodded against his chest, a few tears spilled down my face, but I managed to keep myself from falling apart completely. "Thanks, Dad. I'll be fine, I just need a minute to process he's gone."

He squeezed me tightly once and then left the room, leaving me alone again.

I lay back on the bed, my hands running absently across the top of the comforter as if I'm trying to conjure him back by touching something he had touched.

I shivered, suddenly chilled, and I recalled how warm and safe I had felt when he had joined me in my bed last night. For the very last time. I had a sudden panicked thought I might never be warm again. And it was my fault.

I never should have started this thing between us. I should have made more of an attempt to make things up to Peter, to focus on a relationship with a future. I should have let Kira have her summer fun with Benji, and I should have buried these feelings forever.

Now we were both more broken because of my selfishness. I turned and buried my face into the pillow, smelling Benji's sunshiny pine-soap scent still lingering on the fabric, and my cheeks were hit with tears once more. I had been so sure yesterday that this was the right decision, the only decision. That it was the only way to protect myself from more heartache. Now I was just so cold. Goosebumps rippled across my arms and I shivered between sobs.

He was really gone. And hadn't even said goodbye.

19

"Come on, Desi, stop moping! We are going to have a blast tonight." Eliza clasped my arm and pulled me along the downtown sidewalk toward her favorite local bar. I was just glad Kira wasn't around to insist we go dancing. Clubbing was the last thing I wanted to do.

I groaned, "For you, I will try to have fun tonight."

Meredith had been MIA for the last few weeks with work, Carly and Liam were celebrating Liam's recent promotion, and things were still weird between me and Kira. Thankfully Eliza had taken pity on me after hearing about Benji's abrupt departure and was never one to allow me to wallow.

"I appreciate you trying," she quipped, and we entered the bar and settled into a booth.

We ordered appetizers and giant fruity drinks, and I tried not to think about the gaping hole that appeared in my chest every time I breathed. Eliza had just brought back our third round of drinks when it happened.

"Louis said he gave us double shots for this one!" She rubbed her hands together in glee and I laughed with her, my head already felt a little fuzzy and the hole in my chest seemed smaller.

"Desi Palmer?"

I turned to the sound of my name being called and almost choked on my drink. The tall man closed the distance, a wry smile on his lips as his dark eyes met mine. "Lincoln!"

My grin was wide, and I had enough alcohol in my system that I didn't even bother to hide the fact that I was checking him out. Eliza clutched my arm from across the table and when I turned to look at her, she mouthed *"oh my god"* and I stuck my tongue out at her before Lincoln leaned on our table.

"Fancy meeting you here." He was still dressed to the nines, but the clothing was more casual. Khaki slacks and a crisp, black, v-neck t-shirt. He smelled like expensive cologne and his smile was disarming. It was incredible how easily I had ignored how physically attractive he was before. Then again, before I had been sober. And at work.

I stood and wrapped my arms around him in a hug that was incredibly unprofessional, and Eliza snickered behind me. I was too tipsy to be embarrassed. I stepped back and plopped back into my seat, scooting over to allow Lincoln to join us in the booth. He exchanged pleasantries with Liza, who was doing a shit job at playing it cool, before he returned his attention to me.

"Where's your gentleman this evening?" he asked before he took a sip of his craft beer.

Eliza cleared her throat and made a cutting motion across her chest. I glared at her.

"Oh, that's ended, actually. He's gone back to London," I replied, trying to ignore the hole in my chest threatening to reappear.

"I see." He studied me intensely, and I turned my gaze to Eliza who was waggling her eyebrows at me suggestively. I shook my head at her and rolled my eyes. By the time Lincoln looked across at her, she was engrossed in her phone. "I'm sorry to hear that."

"No, you're not," I teased him, and his lips curved into a small smile, amused by my intoxicated bluntness.

"You're right, I'm not." He took another swig of his drink. "I guess you wouldn't want to take me up on our rain check? Now that you're free to do so?"

"What, right now?" I asked.

"Sure, now works for me." He laughed. "As long as Eliza doesn't mind, that is."

"Oh, that's no problem at all. My boyfriend just sent me a message that he finished up in his shop early tonight anyway," Eliza piped up and I turned and raised an eyebrow at her. Harvey was out of town this weekend. She flashed a toothy grin at me, and I smiled back.

"Okay, well then, sure. I'd love to take you up on the rain check, Lincoln. Just give me a minute to see Eliza off?"

He smiled at me and nodded, standing to let me slide out of the booth.

Eliza was practically buzzing with excitement by the time we made it out the front door. She fanned herself as she gushed.

"My lord, I cannot believe that man is real. He's super into you, Desi!" she squealed and wrapped her tattooed arms around me. I couldn't help but giggle, which made me realize I was a little more intoxicated than I first realized. As if giving a hug to a man I only knew in a professional capacity wasn't a strong enough sign.

"I paid the tab, so you have *fuuuun* with that hunky guy

waiting for you in there." She drew out the word fun as she patted my back before she stepped away.

I hesitated, bringing my eyes up to her icy blue gaze. "I'm not feeling great about this. I mean... Benji and I just ended things, and I jumped into that really quickly after Peter. I feel weird."

Eliza waved off my worries with a flick of her black lacquered fingers. "As far as I'm concerned, this is the perfect opportunity to get over Benji. I know you love him, and I do too, but I cannot see you pining away for him for another eternity before he drops in and blows things up again. You deserve to be happy, Desi. If you don't get a creep vibe from this guy and you feel safe with me leaving, then I don't think you should feel weird about it."

I nodded my head. "You're right. There's nothing wrong with moving on with my life."

"That's the spirit!" she exclaimed before pulling me into a hug again. "Text me when you get home, so I know you made it safely. Or... you know... text me if you don't plan on going home." She waggled her eyebrows at me again.

"I'll text you when I get home, and I'll call you tomorrow to fill you in."

"My girl. Talk to you tomorrow and have fun!" And with that, she disappeared down the street toward her apartment.

I took a deep breath and re-entered the crowded bar. I weaved my way back to where we had left Lincoln. His dark gaze met mine, and I swear my stomach dropped to my toes. A wry smile covered his face, an expression I hadn't seen before in our previous professional encounters, and I couldn't help but smile back.

He leaned in when I reached him to speak directly into my ear. "It's a little loud here. Care to take this to the bar at my hotel down the street?"

I nodded, and he took my hand, leading the way.

We headed two blocks over, and Lincoln explained that he never stays anywhere else when he's in Boston. "I love this location, it's one of the best we have. I'm hoping BHD can elevate what we've done here in the redesigns."

I followed him through the lobby and into the ritzy hotel bar. It was all white and chrome and crystal. Plenty of people milled around and filled the booths and tables scattered throughout the space, but in stark contrast to the bar we'd just come, from most hands were filled with wine glasses and the noise was low enough to carry on a conversation without raising your voice or straining to hear.

Lincoln pointed to a booth in the corner. "Go make yourself comfortable, and I'll grab us both drinks. What's your poison?"

"Gin and tonic, please."

He stopped short and pinned me with his intense gaze. Sizing me up.

"What?" I asked with a light laugh.

He grinned. "You just keep surprising me. I'll be right back"

He turned toward the bar, and I slid into the booth.

He returned, drinks in hand, and slid a plate full of bruschetta across the table. "This place also has great food."

I grabbed a piece of bread from the platter and spooned some of the tomato mixture on top. I took a bite then shot him a thumbs up. It was delicious.

"This place is definitely more your speed," I commented as I looked around the room. "What brought you into the other bar? I can't say I would have ever expected to see you in a place like that."

His cheeks flushed and he looked down at his hands gripping his whiskey glass. "Er... well..."

I cocked my head at him. "Well, what?"

"You're right, it's not my usual scene. I just saw someone I was interested in going through the front door when I was on my way back to my hotel."

"Oh, really? Who was it?" I leaned forward, curious about just who would have made this powerful man go out of his way and out of his comfort zone.

He stared at me pointedly, and it took me a moment too long to realize he meant me.

"Oh." My cheeks flushed.

"I hope that's not too strange. I have thought of you often since we met, and I just thought... maybe if we bumped into each other in a more casual setting..." He shrugged and smiled sheepishly.

I sat back, considering this. For all he'd known, I was still in a relationship with Benji. The thought of the Scotsman made my heart squeeze uncomfortably, so I quickly pushed him out of my mind. I supposed, for Lincoln, calculated risks like following a woman he was interested in into a bar on the off chance her availability may have changed are the sorts of things that made him successful in business.

"No, not too strange." I decided. "I'm glad. This has been a pleasant change of pace for me, honestly."

A welcome distraction from the Benji-sized hole in my life.

We dug into the food and sipped our drinks as we talked. He had a quick wit and an incredibly dry sense of humor that was refreshing. He was obviously intelligent and well-read, but he did an impressive job of not being obnoxious about it. Overall, he was excellent company and a magnetic force of a man. I laughed easily and often.

"So, what are your plans at BHD then? Going to climb

the corporate ladder? I'm sure you'll be running the place before too long." The conversation and sharing of histories had led to him telling me about his meteoric rise to CEO at the ripe age of thirty-one. And now it was my turn.

"This is strictly a personal question, yeah?" I asked, and he nodded back at me eagerly as he leaned forward across the table. "Well, I'm planning to break off on my own as soon as I can. I want to work for myself and build a business that is my own rather than continuing to pour my blood sweat and tears into someone else's baby."

I took a long sip of my gin and tonic and noticed Lincoln stiffen a bit at my words. He shifted from leaning on the table to sitting back against the booth. My eyes widened, and I swallowed quickly. "Shit, I'm sorry. That's kind of exactly what you did, isn't it?"

I was too tipsy for this conversation. Fifteen minutes in and I had already made an ass of myself. A small smile curved his lips and he shook his head at me.

"Don't worry about it. That is exactly what I did, and I don't regret the choices that brought me here. I'm sitting across the table from a beautiful woman..." my next breath caught in my chest at this clear indication that he was, in fact, into me, "...in one of the most luxurious hotels in Boston. When we're done here, I'll go up to the penthouse and enjoy the best suite money can buy."

I laughed at his reference to the penthouse suite, but his dark gaze didn't falter. He wasn't joking, as ridiculous and cheesy as that little speech had been.

"Money doesn't get you everything," I replied, my amusement still playing on my lips.

"It gets you most things," he stated simply.

"There isn't much freedom in climbing the corporate ladder," I said.

He grinned at me, "Once you've gotten high enough up the ladder, the freedom falls into place."

"You still have to answer to investors, right?" I asked. "They could jerk the ladder right out from under you if you rock the boat too much."

He shrugged, "Sure, they could. But at this point I'm far too valuable to them, even if I take risks they don't approve of."

I cocked my head at him, trying to do a serious assessment of this man sitting across from me through the blurry haze of liquor.

"Do you think it's a mistake for me to start my own business?" I was not even sure why I asked this question. Most people thought I was overly ambitious when I shared my goals with them, it wasn't new. Usually, I just brushed it off and ignored the naysayers.

He shook his head. "Not at all. Just a more difficult path. Almost half of all new businesses fail in the first five years." He shrugged, and the flippant way he addressed my life's dream was like a punch to the chest. My eyes narrowed.

"So, you don't think it's a mistake, but you think I'll likely fail within five years?" I retorted.

He widened his eyes and shook his head vigorously, "No, no, that's not what I meant I-"

I held up my hand, cutting him off. "I think it's pretty clear what you meant." I stood, gathering my bag and tossing a few bills on the table as he sat in stunned silence, unable to formulate a response. "For my drink. Thanks for your time, but I should be going."

I turned and stalked toward the hotel lobby. I heard hurried footsteps behind me, and Lincoln's firm hand pressed against my shoulder, "Wait, Desi..."

I spun on my heel, my eyes blazing with an anger I had

felt every single time someone had shit all over my plans. It had all finally boiled over in my semi-drunken state. At this point, I didn't even care that this man was a professional association and that this interaction could have ripple effects for many, many people if he chose to let this encounter affect his business decisions.

"What, Lincoln? What more can you possibly have to say?" I stepped backwards, forcing his hand to fall from my shoulder as I did.

As I stared at his handsome, chiseled face, my dark angry glare meeting his earnest and confused gaze, the only thought in my mind was "*Benji would never doubt me like that.*" And my chest ached as his grinning, freckled face floated into my thoughts.

"I'm sorry, Desi. Can we go back to the table and I can make it up to you? I honestly didn't mean to offend you and I have done just that." His voice was low, there were other people milling around in the lobby after all, and he was sober enough to be concerned about being overheard.

I shook my head. "I don't think that's a good idea. I should go home."

His shoulders slump and he nodded once, his jaw clenched. "Alright, I'll call you a cab."

"Thank you." I sat on a bench near the lobby doors to wait for the cab.

Lincoln ended the phone call and approached me cautiously. "Your car will be here in about five minutes. I really am sorry, Desi. I hope I get a chance to make it up to you."

I just nodded my head once at this second apology. My thoughts still filled with a certain Scottish man who had expressed no inkling of doubt when I had talked about my plans for the future. "Thank you."

When it was clear I would not say anything else, Lincoln turned and soon disappeared into the elevator across the room. Only then did I let my face fall into my hands and allowed the anger to fade into hurt and sadness.

Benji's face still in my head and my heart shattered again across the still healing wounds.

Benji never doubted me.

20

The next week passed in a blur. I was beyond grateful that I was finished with my degree and the Ball-Barlow presentation because I knew my work was suffering right now. I just couldn't focus at the office. I still felt numb and lost, which was the opposite of what I'd been hoping to accomplish upon ending things with Benji.

The point was to have a clean, definite break. No more wondering about what might have been. It was over. He was in London, over three thousand miles away, I was here, and that was that.

My encounter the previous weekend with Lincoln had shaken me. Was the distance really the reason I had ended things? Was it really such a huge barrier? I turned these questions over in my mind each day, trying to find the answer and getting nowhere. How was a relationship, an actual relationship like the one I knew I wanted, supposed to work with so much physical distance?

I crossed paths with Peter a few times at the office. Things were getting a little less awkward between us, but it still wasn't back to the easy flirtatious banter that had filled our encounters previously. I didn't think they would ever get back to that, and that was okay with me. I had truly liked Peter, but after the illuminating conversation I'd had with Lincoln, I knew he wasn't right for me either.

He hadn't been as straightforward with his skepticism as Lincoln, but Peter had ambitions and his eye had always been on climbing the ladder at BHD. He'd always had that little air of "sure, you go ahead and try that" whenever I had mentioned working for myself and carving my own path forward. Always a little condescending glance when I talked about starting my own firm. In retrospect, I now recognized that he didn't truly believe I could do it. He didn't believe in me either.

I knew I needed someone who would go to bat for me. Someone who would be my cheerleader on the rough path I knew was ahead of me as I worked toward building my future. Someone who would pick me up after the inevitable failures, dust me off, and set me forward again. Peter wasn't that person. Lincoln wasn't that person. If Benji couldn't be that person for me either, then I would just have to go it alone until the right person came along.

I made it home after work on Friday, so ready for a weekend to try to come to terms with everything so I could get back on track. I spotted a familiar car in the driveway and my mood brightened. I practically skipped inside and found him in the kitchen, browning up some ground beef at the stove, and I rushed to him, wrapping my arms around his torso and pressing my cheek to his back.

"Agh!" he exclaimed. "Fuck, Desi, you scared the shit out of me." Cyrus laughed and used his free hand to pat my arm gripping his belly.

"You have no idea how happy I am that you're home, Cy," I said and released him, allowing him to return to his task as I settled into a barstool at the counter. "It's been a crazy few months."

"So I've heard," he said, and my cheeks flushed.

"You have?" I asked.

He nodded and opened the spice cabinet. "I have. We don't have to talk about it right now, though, if you don't want to. I'm making tacos, by the way. There will be plenty for you if you want some."

"That sounds great, thanks."

We sat in silence for a few moments as I considered what to say next. I badly wanted to tell Cy everything, but I also didn't want to unload on him completely the moment he returned. He was my baby brother, but with only eighteen months between us, we hadn't grown up with the usual "older sister and younger brother" relationship. We had always been close. I hadn't realized how much I had missed him and his levelheaded, straight forward presence in my life until just now.

"How was Vegas?" I asked, deciding to ease into my personal drama.

"It was amazing. We need to take a trip there together sometime, Des. You'd love it," he replied with a grin. I rolled my eyes. He knew very well that I would enjoy nothing about Las Vegas.

"Ha ha. You're hilarious." I stuck out my tongue at him.

He pointed the spatula at me. "Careful, I may rescind my generous offer to share these tacos."

He returned his attention to the meat in the skillet. It already smelled amazing, and my mouth started to water.

"I think I might have a job lined up there for the fall," he continued. "So you might want to get a little more on board with Vegas if you plan to see me much."

"I'd come to see you, Cy. Don't you worry."

"Good. Now that we've got a tiny update from me out of the way, why don't you tell me what's been going on with you?"

He knew me too well.

"Well, you know Benji was in town this summer?" I asked.

"Was he? News to me," he replied with his usual dead-pan sarcasm.

"You're lucky you are making my dinner, or I'd throw something at you right now." I laughed, "Anyway, Benji was in town and you know we had that weird... *thing*... the last time he was here."

Cy nodded. "Right. He deflowered you and then went back to Scotland and you've been pining after him ever since. Go on."

This statement took me by surprise. "You knew?" I asked.

He turned his attention to me, his eyebrow arched and a "*you're kidding*" expression on his face. "Yes, I knew. You've been in love with that boy since we were kids. And the feelings are mutual. It's pretty obvious to anyone who sees the two of you together."

"No, I mean, you knew we slept together?" I pressed.

"Oh, that. Yeah, Eliza and Kira told me about that. Like right after it happened. I was worried about you at the time. You weren't acting like yourself after Benji went back to Edinburgh. It's not like it was some big secret or that I don't know you have sex, sis."

I was mildly horrified and a little irritated at my friends for gossiping about me behind my back to my brother, but I guessed it was so long ago now it didn't matter. I shrugged it off and continued. He was flitting around the kitchen now, gathering the remaining ingredients for the tacos.

"Anyway, we had this... unfinished business. When he got here in May, it threw me. Much more than I thought it would. I had thought all this time apart would have made those feelings dull. Or that seeing him again would make me realize I had romanticized the whole thing and he wasn't really that great in reality..." I trailed off.

"And you were wrong," he concluded. As though he was stating an obvious fact. He was busy plating our tacos so he didn't look up at me.

I sighed. "Long story short, yes, I was wrong. After about a month we picked back up right where we left off, and it was even better than I imagined it could be."

"So what's the problem?" he asked as he slid my completed plate of tacos across the countertop.

"The problem was exactly what I'm dealing with now. He's gone. He went back to London. And I'm here, without him. Just like last time," I replied.

He chewed a bite of his taco thoughtfully as I picked up my own and took a bite. With my mouth full of food, I gave him a thumbs up. They were delicious.

"You're an idiot, Desi," he said.

I choked on my bite. My eyes widened at this simple statement. I finished chewing and swallowed it quickly so I could properly react to this assertion.

"How do you figure *I'm* the idiot here?" I asked, my tone annoyed.

"He loves you. You love him. It was all perfect and things were going well. Why the fuck would you think the fact that Benji was going back to London would be a real problem?"

His statement was so logical, rational, and devoid of emotion that I couldn't quite wrap my head around it.

"My life is here, Cy," I replied finally.

He shook his head, a small smile appearing on his lips, "No, Desi. Your life is where you make it. If that means it's with Benji, then you go with Benji. What do you really have keeping you here in Boston? What's really stopping you from leaving?"

I hesitated. What was I so afraid of? Why hadn't it occurred to me that I could simply go with him back to London? Why hadn't Benji brought it up?

"But..." I started and couldn't finish the thought. Cyrus looked at me across the counter, his eyebrow now raised incredulously.

"Desi, you're my sister and I love you. But sometimes you lack vision." He filled the silence between bites of food. "It's no wonder you're stuck in a corporate design job right now."

I narrowed my eyes at him. "Fuck off, Cy. You know that's not forever."

He grinned and nodded, "Yeah, I know. Probably better than anyone. But if you don't stop letting fear affect your decisions, your plans are going to become just some dream you used to have when you were young. And a corporate job *will* be your forever."

He was right. I knew he was right. It was fear of failure holding me back. It was why I still hadn't started looking for an apartment even though I'd gotten my big bonus that would easily cover any of the potential expenses I could imagine. Even though I was certain to get a raise after my work on the Ball-Barlow project and could definitely afford it. It was why I had made no concrete plans for my future, no real timeline for when I'd leave BHD and set off on my own.

It was fear that had guided me when I'd ended things with Benji. It was fear that kept me from finding another solution to the distance problem.

"I fucked up, Cy," I said.

"Not beyond repair," he replied. "What matters now is what you do next."

An idea rooted in my head then and a rough plan unfolded.

"I know what I need to do." I shoved the rest of my taco into my mouth, chewing carefully and swallowing before I stood, "Can you help me with something?"

Cy took a dramatic bow, his grin wide across his face. "At your service, as always."

21

*T*hings moved quickly after dinner.

Cyrus booked me a flight to London while I gathered everything I needed, packed a bag, and located my long-unused passport that was luckily still valid. I drafted an email to Jillian letting her know I'd be taking an unexpected trip and would likely not be in the office for the next week at least. I sent the message with only a slight hesitation, only a mild terror for what sort of consequences I would face for not giving notice for this sort of extended leave.

It didn't matter. If everything worked out the way I was hoping, I didn't think I'd be coming back to BHD, anyway.

I hugged Cyrus tightly as we said goodbye in front of the airport, and he whispered in my ear, "I'm so proud of you, sis."

I checked my bank account while I was waiting to board my flight, knowing the balance was about to take a tumble once I paid for the ticket I had charged to my credit card. Doing the mental math, I knew it would still be okay.

It would be okay as long as I was with Benji.

The adrenaline didn't cease until I was finally in my seat

on the airplane. Even then, I found it hard to wind down. Ten o'clock, not even five hours since I had been sitting in my parent's kitchen eating tacos with my brother.

I found the address of the restaurant while on the plane. The red-eye flight gave me plenty of time to sleep, though it was broken and fitful. At the very least, it kept me from dwelling and overthinking this decision for hours. I was eerily calm about this very impulsive, very out of character thing that I was doing, and deep down I knew that meant this was right.

It was around ten o'clock the following morning when I approached the hostess inside the London restaurant that was already bustling with Saturday brunch traffic. I had to wait a few minutes behind a line of eager diners. My hands shook in anticipation.

Finally, she turned her hospitable grin to me. "How can I help you today?"

"I'm looking for Benji?"

Her smile faltered a bit and her eyebrows wrinkled in confusion. "Benji? I'm sorry; he's not here anymore. Is there someone else who can help?"

My head was spinning now. The whole reason he had come back to London last month was for Hank and his job at this restaurant. The whole reason he had left me. And he wasn't here?

"Um... no. This is personal, actually. Do you know where I could find him?" Awkward. So awkward. I wished I had a phone number where I could reach him. Social media seemed such an impersonal way to have this conversation.

"One moment." She smiled and disappeared to the back room.

A moment later a familiar large man appeared in front of me. His eyes widened a bit in surprise, but he grinned and embraced me. "Desi! What a pleasant surprise." He turned and nodded to the hostess. She returned to her work as he pulled me aside to sit at a table in the corner. "What brings you all the way across the pond, then?"

I cleared my throat. My cheeks flushed a bit. "I need to talk to Benji. And I need to do it in person."

He nodded, studying me carefully. Taking in my slightly disheveled appearance and the circles under my eyes. "I think I can help you with that. But first, I need to be sure of something." I nodded and waited for him to continue. "I need to be sure you aren't here to break his heart again."

My chest tightened at this statement, but I remained silent. It didn't seem that Hank was finished.

"Benji is like a son to me. When he came back from Boston... well, I don't think I've ever seen him that low. Ever. He didn't say as much, but I'm thinking it has something to do with you based on how close the two of you were when I visited."

My throat closed up and tears stung my eyes. I fought to keep them from spilling out. I hadn't wanted to hurt him. I nodded once more, affirming Hank's thoughts on the matter.

"I see. If you are here to make it right, then I'll tell you where to find him. Otherwise, I'm afraid I can't help you." He leaned back, clasping his hands together at his belly as he waited for a response.

"I screwed up, Hank. I'm here to clean up my mess," I replied as a few tears broke loose from my lashes. Thankfully, my voice remained steady. Even if inside I felt like I was about to fall apart.

"Good." He pulled a pen and a pad of paper out of his apron and scrawled on it. He handed me the paper and I read it, my own eyes widening a bit as Hank let out a chuckle at my reaction. "I guess giving him a bit of freedom also gave him the confidence to follow his dreams." Hank shrugged. "As I said, he's like a son to me. I want him to succeed. And I know he will, which is why I made the business investment as well."

Written on the paper was the address and name of Benji's bakery in Edinburgh, Scotland.

THE TRAIN RIDE to Edinburgh was worse than the plane ride from Boston. My mind would not quit spinning, and my adrenaline never really slowed after my short meeting with Hank at the restaurant in London. Hearing that Benji hadn't been quite himself since his return had shaken me. Maybe I had fucked things up even worse than I thought. Maybe after all of this - this very Benji-esque impulsive gesture - he would turn me away.

Maybe it was over for him.

My hands shook, and I fought to calm myself during the six-hour trip. I closed my eyes and breathed deeply, gripping tightly to the small bag on my lap. The only luggage I'd brought with me. I had picked up a book in the train station, but it sat next to me on the seat. I couldn't seem to focus on the words and right now the last thing I wanted to do was read about some other not-as-stupid-as-me heroine's happy ending. Especially when my own was still hanging in such a tenuous balance.

Somehow, with my head leaned back against the seat and my eyes closed and my focus on my breathing, I fell asleep. When I woke, we were pulling into the station in Scotland.

I looked up the address before I exited the train, and the bakery was within walking distance. Fifteen minutes, according to GPS. I needed the air anyway. I needed to get my thoughts together. I needed to stop this fucking incessant tremble threatening to bring me to my knees with each step.

My pace was quicker than I had intended and in a few minutes, I was standing across the street from the shop. The sign was already in place. "Benji's Bread & Bakery"; a brilliant bold yellow font outlined in black. Very Benji. Beneath the sign hung a white banner that had "Grand Opening - September 25th" splashed across in bright red. He had really done it. This was his dream and here it was, nearly a reality. Next weekend and all the pieces would be in place.

I smiled for a moment before remembering why I was here, and my heart started up again at a frantic pace. I stepped back and collapsed onto a bench, my eyes never leaving the doorway.

It was nearing 7pm. Maybe he wasn't even here. I finally got my breathing back under control when I heard the bell tinkle above the door across the street. A familiar shape emerged, followed by a lithe, fair, and freckled red-headed girl. They were laughing, though I couldn't hear what they were saying. The wind carried their voices down the street. Benji turned to lock the door and then back to the red-head, leaning to give her a big hug as he whispered something in her ear. She grinned and kissed him on the cheek before turning to head up the street. He stood and watched her go until she disappeared around the corner.

I was frozen in place. My breathing had stopped entirely, and my throat had tightened beyond what I thought was possible.

Once the girl disappeared, Benji turned to head the

opposite direction. At first, I thought he wouldn't see me at all. That I'd be able to escape this with my dignity intact. He would never need to know I was here. Hank would tell him about our meeting earlier today, maybe. But he could just assume I'd gone home then. That I hadn't made a complete fool of myself by coming all the way here just to discover he had moved on. That it was over.

My worst fears came to pass.

He did a double-take.

His hazel gaze fell on me across the street on the bench and he squinted his eyes as if he couldn't quite believe what he was seeing. That maybe it was a trick of the light that I was actually sitting here on a bench across from his bakery in Scotland. My cheeks flushed as his eyes widened, but I still could not bring myself to move.

"Desi?" he called as he started across the street. "Desi. What are you... how did you...?"

I felt the tears spring to my eyes, and I hated myself for being such a crybaby. It was a mixture of grief, embarrassment, and a strange relief at seeing him. He was here, right here. In a moment, I would be able to reach out and touch him. I hadn't realized until this very moment just how viscerally I had missed him.

My throat was still closed up so I couldn't answer him. I just shrugged, my eyes meeting his as he rubbed at his face in disbelief. He lowered himself onto the bench next to me and, somehow, I stopped myself from reaching out to him. I came all this way and now I was mute. I cleared my throat and took a deep breath. I nodded in the direction the red-head had disappeared.

"She's cute," I said simply.

He turned his face to mine, his brow wrinkled in confusion. "Huh?"

I pointed to the corner where she'd disappeared. "The girl that just left. She's cute."

He shook his head. "Six weeks, three thousand miles, and the only thing you have to say is my bakery manager is cute?"

Relief flooded me then, and the tears spilled down my face. He reached out to me, his warm grip on my elbow was comforting.

"Hey, it's alright, lass," he soothed.

"I'm sorry, Benji. I'm so sorry. I thought... well... I thought it was really done. I had really fucked everything up this time and you'd moved on and I came all this way for nothing and-"

The words came spilling out, but before I could continue my rambling, he grabbed my face in both his long-fingered hands and kissed me so deeply that I lost the ability to breathe again.

My bag fell from my lap as I wrapped my arms around his neck and pressed myself against him like the only thing that could save me was his touch. His hands moved from my face to my waist as he pulled me onto his lap.

He broke the kiss and nuzzled his face into the curls at my neck. "I can't believe you're really here." He squeezed me tightly, placing soft kisses at my collar bone as he inhaled deeply. I ran my nails across his scalp, and he turned his face up to mine again, his eyes glistening and wet.

"I'm here. And I am not going anywhere," I whispered.

"I won't survive it if you do," he replied.

"Never again. I promise you. Right here is where I've always needed to be."

EPILOGUE

"*N*o, no. This is bad, Desi. You should have called me sooner." Carly shook her head, frowning.

"Well, can you help?" I asked.

"It's going to be tough, but I can help. I'll get some inspo boards started and send them over to you ASAP," she replied seriously.

I turned the camera on my phone back to show my face. "You're a lifesaver. Between helping Benji get the bakery ready for the opening and getting all the paperwork together to be able to stay here in Edinburgh, I haven't had a single second to consider what to do with the apartment."

Benji had been living here for several weeks before I joined him in Scotland, but still the place looked bare, blank, and clinical. It was stressing me out that our first place together still didn't feel like home. So, I'd called Carly for help. Residential design was her specialty, after all.

"I'm so glad you called me. It's got potential, for sure, and this way I get to see your beautiful face on video chats on the regular." She grinned. "We miss you already, babe."

"I miss you guys too. We will be back for Christmas though! Just a few months away," I replied.

"Can't wait!" she squealed.

I heard the front door open. "Oh! Benji's home. Don't want to ruin the surprise so I'll talk to you later, okay?"

"Sure thing. Love you, Desi, talk soon!" She blew me a kiss, and I ended the call just as Benji made his way into the living room.

He wrapped his arms around my waist and buried his nose in my curls, inhaling deeply. He kissed my neck and then his hot breath tickled my ear as he whispered, "It still doesn't feel real that you're here."

I turned to face him; my arms wound around his neck and I pressed myself to him. "What should I do to make it feel more real?"

He grinned, and that lopsided smile still made my stomach flip.

"I can think of a few things, but maybe best to discuss in the bedroom." His eyes twinkled, and he nodded to the large window that overlooked the street below. "Or at least close the curtains."

"Oh, a private discussion then?" I asked.

"Very private." His hands on my hips, his long fingers dipped below the top of my jeans. Then, in a swift movement, he bent and scooped me off my feet. I giggled as he carried me down the hall toward our bed in our apartment that was soon going to feel like home.

I was finally where I was always supposed to be.

THE END

If you enjoyed Desi and Benji's story, be sure to check out Carly and Liam's relationship origins in my free novella, My Only Exception! Get your copy today when you sign up for my author newsletter.

ACKNOWLEDGMENTS

I hope you loved taking this journey with Desi and Benji as much as I did! These two are definitely very near and dear to my heart. I couldn't have finished this book during the chaos that was the year of 2020 without the help of the following *awesome* people who spent their time and energy to help me shape the story into its best possible form.

Every friend and family member who has expressed their support and excitement for this endeavor into self-publishing.

Kacey, Tera, Michelle, Jessi, Melissa, and Nicole for being willing beta readers. Your encouragement, enthusiasm, and feedback were instrumental for finishing this work!

Everyone in EC for helping me sift through a million different versions of book covers trying to find the perfect one (fonts are the bane of my existence).

Beth at Magnolia Author Services for her patience working with an overly enthusiastic and anxious first-time author and for her wonderfully professional editing and formatting! Thanks for cleaning up all of my weak areas and polishing the details so the story could shine.

Finally, a special thanks to my husband for his unending support including reading a *very* rough draft of this story despite not being much of a reader in general. He's my biggest supporter and inspiration in most areas of my life. Thank you so much for all you do for myself and our family.

ABOUT THE AUTHOR

Jessa Harmon is a lifetime lover of storytelling. From the first "book" she wrote as a fifth grader in a simple spiral notebook, she knew that she loved writing stories to share with others.

As an author, her passion is bringing to life diverse and genuine characters navigating real relationships. Her contemporary romance novels have heart, but they aren't lacking in steam.

When she's not writing she enjoys reading a wide variety of genres, watching feel-good movies, spending time with loved ones, cooking, good wine and good coffee. She unashamedly loves puns, dad jokes and witty memes.

Keep up with Jessa on one of the following platforms!

Website ➜ www.jessaharmon.com
Facebook ➜ www.facebook.com/JessaHarmonBooks
Instagram ➜ www.instagram.com/jessaharmon/
Sign up for her newsletter for a free novella and to be notified of new releases! ➜ www.jessaharmon.com/newsletter/

Printed in Great Britain
by Amazon